WAVES END

Also by C.W. Irwin

Society of the Morning Star

Waters of Eden

WAVES END

C.W. Irwin

For Rhonda

1

 as icy water pulls you from the edge of oblivion. It tastes salty, like ocean water, and you are stunned to discover that you're lying on your back, sprawled on wet sand. Another breaker foams around you with a hissing sound, the silken bubbles caressing your naked skin. Pushing yourself up onto your elbows, you gaze at the series of waves rolling toward you, expecting to see the wreckage of a ship bobbing up and down in the surf—a beached hull, a broken mast, splintered lifeboats. But there's no wreckage of any kind out there. There's only the churning surf and glittering stars …

Even after your mind clears a bit, a hole remains where your identity used to be: you can't remember who you are, much less how you got here. When the ocean delivered you back to land, it apparently washed the slate of your memory clean.

It is night and all is eerily quiet. On a high promontory not far down the beach, the unlit eye of an ancient lighthouse towers over this edge of land and the dark silhouette of a large building looms behind you, facing the endless breakers. Sand dunes have drifted over a low seawall and onto a cracked macadam street identified by a rusted sign reading OCEAN AVENUE. Unwinding a ribbon of cellophane-like seaweed from your ankles, you attempt to walk but your legs feel like rubber and you immediately collapse. You try again, and fall again. Finally regaining a modicum of equilibrium, you stagger across the beach to one of the dunes that spilled over the seawall. There you carefully slide down the loose sand to the macadam. No traffic is approaching from either direction. In fact, no vehicles are visible anywhere … just a line of dark streetlights. A sidewalk borders the other side of the street, and beyond it a flagstone walkway winds through a small yard to the entrance of the dark building.

This building is a sprawling three-story Victorian structure flanked by two side wings and numerous balconies, painted white with green shutters—a gingerbread fantasy of turrets, spokes, and wooden tracery. A huge rusted anchor lies on the yellow grass in the front yard, as though anchoring the sky, and bolted to the mansard roof a faded sign proclaims: CAPTAIN'S QUAY HOTEL. No lights glow in any of the windows. Except for the sighing of the wind and the whisper of the surf, no other sound ripples through the still air—not even the primitive language of dogs.

Standing there on the cold street, you discover that it is hard to link words together into a coherent train of thought. It feels like the space inside your mind merged with the vast space outside, the defining boundary between them gone.

Sagging steps creak under your feet as you climb to the front veranda. A heavy door with cut-glass windows opens onto a hushed lobby, where brocaded sofas and chairs, all covered with a thick layer of dust, stand in a neat array on a threadbare carpet. The walls here are strangely bare—no portraits of serious-looking men wearing black ties and wing collars, no glossy oil paintings of tall sailing ships. Just one mirror with beveled edges and a few unlit gaslights with a fringe of crystal prisms hanging beneath them. Everything looks more than a hundred years old.

"Hello," you call out, "is anyone here?

An echo is the only reply: *is … anyone … here … here … here …*

Suddenly conscious of your nakedness, you duck behind the reception desk, leaving only your face visible to anyone who might enter the lobby. The desk's broad surface is clear except for a call bell and a guestbook. You slam the button on the bell repeatedly, but the motionless air in the lobby quickly swallows up the intrusive *ding … ding … ding.* No one appears—no bell captain, no concierge, no other guests. Apparently you're alone here. What's more, the hotel doesn't seem to have a telephone. In fact, the place looks like it was abandoned long ago.

At this point you become aware of something else extremely odd: even though no sun or moon illuminates this scene, you can somehow *see.* A sepulchral half-light suffuses everything, but the source of this dim light is nowhere to be found. As insane as it sounds, it's as though you are somehow illuminating this place with your eyes.

Leaving the reception desk, you venture into the wide hallway beyond the lobby. It smells musty from mildew, which has left its brown signature on the faded wallpaper. Two long rows of wooden doors, all enameled dark green, face each other across the corridor. The door of the first guestroom clicks open easily.

This room is furnished in a Spartan fashion—just a simple oak dresser, a wooden chair, and a sea chest at the foot of a narrow bed. Curiously, however, an assortment of antique nautical instruments occupies the top of the dresser: a compass, an ancient Ulysse-Nardin chronometer, and a tarnished brass sextant that someone may have once used to follow a star. Next to the sextant lies a three-inch piece of leather strap, cracked and frayed at one end, as though it had broken off someone's belt.

The sea chest looks like it survived from an earlier century—barrel top and sturdy sides of varnished wood, its corners reinforced with caps of wrought iron. When you lift its lid, a plume of cedar fragrance unfolds in the room. A sea captain's jacket lies neatly folded at the bottom of it. Strangely enough, this garment is not frayed or moth-eaten. In fact, it looks brand new, the brass buttons still shiny. This seafarer's coat could be significant, for on one wall of the room a yellowed nautical chart sags where the damp air weakened the glue fastening it to the wallpaper. The map features an inlet in a serpentine coastline. Lines of latitude and longitude crisscross the image, but no numbers appear on them and no name identifies the showcased inlet. The needle in the compass on the dresser points to North, implying that the hotel faces East. Okay ... but who knows what the words "North" and "East" mean here?

The air in the room feels chilly, so you take out the old captain's jacket and put it on, buttoning up the front. It hangs a bit loosely from your shoulders, but you're grateful for its woolen warmth, so you keep it on. Folded beneath the jacket you find a pair of gabardine pants and you climb into them. Luckily, they also fit. You even find a pair of boots under the bed, and slip these on as well.

The guestroom next door is almost identical to the first one—simple dresser, bed, and ladder-backed chair—but with no sea chest, no nautical chart, no navigational instruments. And no sign of a recent guest.

The room directly across the hall from this one is no different; in fact, all the rooms on this floor look pretty much the same.

A broad staircase leads to the upper two floors, where similar rooms with similar furniture also reveal no evidence of recent habitation. A three-legged table stands at the end of the top hallway, displaying a vase containing a spray of wilted flowers. The slightest touch makes the blossoms crumble to dust.

The unsettling truth is: this old building feels more like a mausoleum than a hotel.

Shivering, you descend the stairs and return to the first guest room. Breakers whisper outside the hotel, as though trying to lull you to sleep:

Shhhh …. shhhh …

Lying down on the bed, you pull the bedspread over you and sink into a bottomless sleep as waves lap rhythmically at the edge of land.

2

IT IS STILL DARK WHEN YOU WAKE UP, BUT AS FAR AS YOU'RE CONCERNED a new day has just dawned, since your circadian sleep cycle appears to be the only calendar available here. It's far from an exact system, but it works after a fashion. Period of wakefulness: day. Period of sleep: night. And who knows, it may even be more reliable than the childishly simple grids printed on commercial calendars.

The single window in the room is wide open, its lace curtain billowing in a cool breeze that is fresh with the briny fragrance of seawater and kelp. The breeze, with its tantalizing promise of open space and freedom, beckons you.

Okay then … right … time to find out exactly where this place is …

The hotel lobby is still deserted and quiet as a tomb. Once again, you call out: "Hello? Hello? Is anyone here?" But once again, no one replies.

Where IS this place? What the hell is going on here?

Rows of brass keys hang on a board behind the reception desk. Only one is missing—the one to room 101, the room where you spent the night. But that's odd … you don't remember taking the key. You didn't need it; the door to your room was unlocked.

A large guest book—a folio-sized volume bound in black Morocco—lies splayed open on the desk. No names appear on its pages, however. All of them are as blank as your memory.

The veranda provides a good view of the small crescent-shaped beach out front, but no evidence of a shipwreck has yet materialized—no bodies sprawled on the sand like wet rag dolls, no sign of any other people anywhere, dead or alive. Just the smooth gray sand and the white mosaic fragments of sea shells.

The promontory down the beach promises to be an even better vantage point, so you trudge toward it across the soft dunes. Breakers slap the foot of the outcropping as you clamber up the slippery rocks forming its steep sides.

The level space on top does indeed provide a panoramic view of the coastline and the checkerboard grid of streets etched beside the ocean. Except for the encroaching dunes, all the streets are vacant—not a single person or vehicle in sight.

And even from this highest elevation in the immediate area, you don't see any lights glowing anywhere—no welcoming lamps in cottage windows, no jewel-like ship's lanterns sparkling on the horizon. Even the huge Fresnel lens at the top of the lighthouse tower is nothing more than a dead crystal now, no longer any help to sailors.

A veil of cool mist glazes your face and the breeze meandering over the flat water caresses your cheeks, teasing you with the exhilarating fragrance of ocean air and surf—a hint of something that feels like freedom. But it is a cruel breeze, for it offers that tantalizing clue but no answers — certainly no answer to the most important questions of all: *who are you and how did you get here?*

The lighthouse keeper's cottage hugs the base of the tower. It is hard to see through its salt-smeared casement windows, but the room inside looks stark — a still life of whitewashed walls and a simple wooden table and chair … no lighthouse keeper, no radio, no maps. An ancient, massive padlock hangs from the door handle. Years of sea spray have turned its laminated iron into layers of malachite-and-turquoise-colored corrosion, as though it had hung for centuries on the door of a sunken ship. It doesn't budge, and no one comes to answer when you pound on the door.

Frustrated, you pick up a rock and shatter one of the panes of glass in the window. Reaching through the jagged breach, however, you discover that the metal latch is rusted firmly shut. This lighthouse — like the town next to it — seems to have been abandoned many years ago.

An array of old tombstones, pitted and leaning precariously, occupies a square of tangled grass in front of the lighthouse. Pale green lichens encrust the stones and the inscriptions on them are worn so smooth they're illegible. But as bleak and melancholy as this scene is, the lighthouse — this dark eye asleep at the edge of the Earth — seems to harbor a secret within its glass, for the mere sight of it instills in you a sensation of immense age — ancientness beyond measure — as though this former scepter of light were a cenotaph to a long-vanished god.

The power of this intuition leaves you spellbound for a moment, standing there staring at the tower as though hypnotized. Even after the bizarre feeling fades, it leaves in its wake the residual suspicion that, in some strange way, this lighthouse must be very important.

Of course, another explanation would be that this strange feeling — this primordial aura that you sensed — is simply a deeply submerged hope that the lighthouse contains a hidden magical power, that it will burst back to life one day, its gleaming sword of light slashing through the darkness, laying everything bare before you.

But for now the old bones below your feet mark the farthest boundary of everything you know and maybe everything you will ever know …

Before long, the gentle breeze tousling your hair morphs into a blustering wind, propelling waves that crash and spatter over the jagged rocks at the foot of the bluff. A storm seems to be brewing over the ocean … a good time to return to the hotel.

Down on the dunes, however, a strange phenomenon occurs. For a moment, everything — the beach, the ocean, the hotel — takes on a smoky-red hue and becomes filmy, translucent. This illusion lasts just a few seconds, however, like a flash of summer lightning. Then everything returns to normal. That is, if the word "normal" has any meaning here …

An old saying now echoes in your mind: *Red sky at night, sailors' delight … red sky at morning, sailors take warning …*

But is this morning or night? How can you tell?

The dissolved granules of primeval Pangaea — the last supercontinent to break apart — feel cold under your feet as you stride across the sand.

3

WHEN THE UNIVERSE EMERGED FROM THE VAST RESERVOIR OF TIMELESS space, could it have emerged many-sided—with sunlit sides and shady sides, visible sides and hidden sides? That theory would explain a lot: you may have just stumbled into one of the hidden sides, a side where the sun never rises and the Moon never shines. Are there shadow-people in this shadow-land, or are you the only one here?

The gigantic ocean is stirring now. Powerful waves pound the jetties with a sound like muffled thunder and the clouds overhead suddenly light up as though flashbulbs were popping off behind them. Zigzag lightning bolts arc from the bottom of the clouds to the glossy surface of the ocean. Then a minor miracle happens: a dim glow glimmers in the streetlamps along Ocean Avenue. The blue circus dog of electricity has returned, once again performing tricks inside the glass globes! Unfortunately, this impromptu performance doesn't last long. Seconds later, the lamps wink out and all is dark again. All is still.

A crooked trail of footprints leads from the edge of the water to the seawall in front of the hotel. For a second your hopes soar: *has someone else arrived?* But when you insert your right foot into one of the impressions in the sand, it fits perfectly. So it's yours then … there's still no sign that anyone else has checked in at the Captain's Quay Hotel.

But another surprise awaits you inside.

A smoky fragrance suffuses the air in the lobby. For a panicky second you're afraid that the hotel caught on fire, but that is not the case; the smoke is coming from a fire crackling in the fireplace. A film of violet flame wraps around the oak logs stacked neatly on the andirons and the wood hisses occasionally, emitting puffs of fragrant smoke from the ends of the logs.

That fire wasn't lit before. Someone else MUST be here …

You run to the front desk and examine the guestbook. Sure enough, a name has appeared on the first page.

Although you still can't remember your own name, you're pretty sure this one isn't it, for you know very well that you didn't attempt to sign in when you arrived. It's the name "Ryder", written on the top line in florid handwriting, with decorative loops of varying thickness, as though someone penned the name using a metal crow-quill pen dipped in an old-fashioned inkwell.

Did this Ryder person light the fire?

The mantelpiece is bare except for a thick layer of dust—no matches, no lighter, not even a blackened stick of wood that someone might have used to ignite the kindling. Using an iron poker to sift through the ashes below the logs, you find no remains of matches there either, or anything else that could have started the fire.

Perplexed, you return to the desk and examine the guestbook again, turning the brittle pages one by one. But the name "Ryder"—penned flamboyantly on the first page—is still the only name in the book.

Is someone named Ryder using this guestbook to communicate with you? If so, it might be a good idea to reply …

One of the drawers in the desk contains a pen and a small bottle of ink. The pen is an impressive piece of Victorian craftsmanship, with a mother-of-pearl handle and a fine-pointed silver nib. Oddly enough, though, the ink is crimson. You flip open the metal lid of the bottle and dip the pen into the ink. But as soon as you start to write, things go crazy. The pen starts to move on its own, as though your hand were obediently following it across the page.

You've heard of "automatic writing" before but never thought it would be like this! The pen isn't even writing legible words. It's just scratching out a line of unintelligible scrawl …

Startled, you drop the pen and the red ink spatters dramatically across the page. Ringing the desk bell repeatedly does nothing but fracture the silence; nobody responds to its summoning. Then, when you turn away from the desk, your heart stops for an instant.

A girl is standing in the hallway, staring at you. She looks like she's maybe ten or twelve years old, with a pale face, large sparkling eyes, long blond hair, and wearing a plain white linen dress.

"H-hello," you manage to stammer. "You scared me! I didn't know anyone else was here."

The girl doesn't move. She just stands there in the gloom, frozen, gazing at you with a penetrating stare.

"Is your name 'Ryder'?" you ask in a friendly tone.

She doesn't respond … doesn't even blink an eye.

"Can't remember your name? I can't remember mine either. Funny, isn't it?"

She moves her mouth as though saying something but you don't hear anything.

"I think I was shipwrecked," you tell her. "How did *you* get here? Were you shipwrecked too?"

She is still staring at you, as though studying your face. Then you hear her say something. Well, "hear" may not be the right word ... her voice sounds like it's echoing inside your skull.

Will you play hide and seek with me? the voice says.

"Who are you?"

She disappears in an instant.

"No, don't go!" you exclaim. "I want to talk with you."

I'm over here ...

Swiveling around, you see her face in the mirror hanging on the far wall. But she is not standing in front of it. She is not standing anywhere in the room.

"Wow ... that's a neat trick—"

Do you know who I am?

"Is your name 'Ryder'?"

She shakes her head.

"Then who are you? Please ... tell me."

She giggles and the image in the mirror vanishes.

The only trace of her that remains is lilting, disembodied laughter. Racing down the hallway, you open the doors one by one and peer into the rooms, but there's no one there.

Next, you run upstairs, checking those rooms as well. It takes only minutes to search every room on the second and third floors, but there's no one in the hotel but you.

Gazing through a large Palladian window in the top floor, you survey the dark buildings of the town, searching for a light signaling human habitation. But there's nothing outside but dark roofs and shadowy spires.

Back in the lobby, the mirror where the girl's face appeared moments ago now frames a very ordinary reflection of the lobby—a crushing disappointment that leaves behind a wisp of pain twisting deep inside your head. And outside, no new footprints have appeared on the sand.

Who was that girl?

The quill pen is still lying on the reception desk, next to the guestbook. Dipping it gingerly in the crimson ink, you touch the point to the paper. This time it doesn't move on its own. You scrawl the words:

I am in room 101. Please contact me. I want to talk with you.

Heart pounding with anticipation, you sit on a leather wing chair facing the front door of the hotel. The thought that someone else may have arrived to share this nightmare with you is exciting, but at the same time worrisome. Who is this girl anyway? And if she's a ghost, is that altogether a good thing? Are all ghosts benevolent? Of course, what are the memories of deceased people if not ghosts? Maybe you, too, are a ghost—a disembodied Ego flitting through these halls like a shadow.

Could that be what you are now? A ghost? Dreaming that you're a live person?

A gust of wind whistles over the dunes. As bright tongues of flame continue to lick at the logs in the fireplace, another question surfaces in your mind: if *she's* not Ryder, then who is? Who wrote that name in the guestbook? Are there *numerous* ghosts here?

So you wait. What else can you do?

The fire continues to crackle and hiss and the wind off the ocean begins to howl. But no one enters the hotel. Despite the inclement weather, no one comes in from the night, and the girl-ghost does not reappear.

Come on! Someone must have set that fire! Someone real …

4

TIME HERE FEELS BOTH SUSPENDED AND DESPERATELY IMPORTANT, LIKE the time between heartbeats. Both hands on the mantel clock in the lobby are frozen at "12". With your index finger pressed firmly on your wrist, you've counted 3,680 heartbeats since you sat down on the wing chair in the lobby—about one hour.

And even though you've added no wood to the fire, it shows no sign of going out. Now and then, pockets of sap in the logs pop loudly and orange sparks fly up into the flue.

But the strange little girl still hasn't returned. No one—person or spirit—has emerged from the night. As you wait there, patiently listening to the fire and the wind, your thoughts spiral back to the huge moment when you woke up on the beach outside—your point of entry into these ghost latitudes, azimuth and declination unknown. Studying the stars would be useless; the constellations look totally unfamiliar.

The most terrifying reality of all is: *you still can't remember who you were before you came here. You can't even remember how you got here. It's not like you used some sort of magic sextant. Did you just sleepwalk into this place?*

Maybe you mentally escaped a devastating life event by slipping into a classic fugue state, full-blown, accompanied by amnesia. But if that is what this is, what happened? What caused this nightmare? No idea. No clues emerge, no palimpsests from a former life. You aren't even sure you *want* to remember, for your amnesia may be shielding you from a trauma so horrific that just remembering it could destroy you.

You imagine that even now, as you sit in this abandoned hotel, Druids of Geography on the Other Side are trying to figure out where you went. But this is no doubt a delirious fantasy. In all likelihood no one is looking for you. Why would they? At this point your thoughts probably don't possess enough energy to penetrate the boundary of your Egosphere, as though you had fallen into some sort of mental black hole *(now where did that thought come from?)*

In any case, one thing seems abundantly clear: if you're going to get out of here, you first need to know how you *got* here, for it is reasonable to assume that the way in is also the way out. And if you can't find the way out, you could be stranded here forever.

•   •   •

Your eyelids grow heavy as you sit in the lobby, and sleep begins to pull you under as flames curl around the logs in the hearth and the wind continues to howl and still no one comes in through the door. And the only light in the room is the eerie luminescence that seems to emanate from within everything, along with the prehistoric light of the flames dancing in the hearth.

But then a sudden noise jars the silence. It sounds like a door. The girl? Ryder?

"Who's there?"

Another banging sound echoes from the far end of the hall. You bound over the creaking floorboards of the corridor, trying each door you pass. All of them are still unlocked, and all of them are still empty.

"Hello!" you yell. "Ryder? Is that you? Where are you?"

More silence for a minute, then another BANG …

At the shadowy end of the long hallway a loose shutter is swinging in the wind, occasionally slamming against the window frame. After securing the latch on it, you return heavy-hearted to the lobby. You may simply have to accept the fact that the hotel is open, a fire is burning in the fireplace, and that's all there is to it. By now you've learned that this place has its own peculiar logic—like how you don't seem to need food and can see in the dark. No use in trying to figure it out.

Back in your room, nothing has changed; the oak dresser is still there, along with the bed and the chair and the mysterious sea chest with its forest-fragrance of cedar. Everything seems to be in order.

But then the room starts spinning.

The molecules of your body, with their magnetic thoughts, suddenly feel weightless, and you're afraid you're about to drift away like a memory being forgotten. The feeling is oddly familiar; something like this may have happened just before you woke up on the beach. Filling your lungs with fresh ocean air, you sit on the edge of the bed and wait. The lightheadedness passes. You feel solid again.

5

AT SOME POINT IN THE INDETERMINATE PAST, A NIGHT WITHOUT EDGES swallowed up this little seaside town. It's easy to visualize how it must have gone down: shadow-puppets on the amusement pier vanishing at sunset, enameled horses on a carousel shuddering to a stop, and vacationers disappearing as soon as they took off their sunglasses. And then: the land sank into preternatural stillness … nothing to hear but the sound of the surf.

When did this catastrophe take place? Hard to tell. You don't even know how long you've been here — it could be two days, maybe more. It's difficult to figure out since you still haven't come across a single clock that works. At some point the hands on all of them came to rest on "12", as though Time itself had crystallized. Of course the hands of clocks never *were* much help to you … all they ever do is spin around in insane circles. And it's not just the clocks here that are weird: the sun still hasn't appeared. Apparently, on this oblique mental surface, it's night all the time. No, not exactly "night". It's a faintly luminous twilight you're tempted to call "daynight". The truth is: you'd sell your soul to see one more incandescent dawn.

Back in the little cemetery by the lighthouse, you sit on one of the marble slabs and try hard to make sense of things. For some reason, this melancholy place helps you think. Maybe it's because of the eerie peacefulness that reigns here; even the seagulls circle over the gravestones in silence, as though lost in their private dreams of sea and sky.

Lingering above the buried chests of ivory, you can't help feeling an odd kinship with the people here — their eye sockets filled with dirt, roots wrapped around pale wrists, restraining them, anchoring them to the Earth. Long ago their spark of life passed on to thoughtless grass and indolent worms as countless raindrops washed the tombstones smooth.

6

THE VERTICAL RIVER OF TIME MEANDERS SLOWLY WHERE IT JOINS THE ocean. There may even be eddies in the current here, deep still pools of Time, but if there are, they are invisible, hidden from sight. Given the age of the buildings in this town, you wonder if you fell backwards into some sort of Time trap concealed in the structure of the universe. Or maybe Time itself slipped along a fault line of some sort. Could it be that you are now standing outside of "normal" Time? That's a very unsettling thought ...

Dare you think the unthinkable?

Did you die?

If you *are* dead this is a very peculiar afterlife, for there is nothing ordinary about a place where the sun never appears above the horizon. It is as though the Earth had turned on an axis you never knew existed.

Your rational, clockwork mind is warning you that you should eat something, but since you still don't feel hungry, something other than food must be sustaining you. It's just as well, for you haven't come across a trace of food anywhere. It could be that the wave-tossed souls who wind up in this harbor aren't supposed to stay long. But if food and water aren't sustaining you, then what is?

The sun is the ultimate source of energy, of course. Its power becomes trapped in plants, making its way into the food chain, into coal, into gasoline. But there is no sun here … or if there is one, it's not energizing this part of the Earth. Maybe that's why you don't need food. You could be metabolizing some other kind of energy, and possibly an abrupt switch from sunlight to this other kind of energy is what disrupted your memory. If so, that would have far-reaching implications, for understanding this phantom energy could be the key to harnessing it. It could even furnish the power to escape.

Escape …

All right, sure … good idea. But escape from where? You still have no idea where you are.

You take a deep breath and head for the door.

It's time to find out …

Three possible routes present themselves: up the coast, down the coast, and inland. For starters, you choose inland. Steeled by new resolve, you leave the hotel, stepping down to the flagstone path that winds through the tawny grass to Ocean Avenue. From the Avenue, you turn left into the grid of vacant streets.

Most of the houses lining these streets look like they were built during the nineteenth century, like the Captain's Quay Hotel. Their windows are dark holes now and many of their doors hang open on rusted hinges. Weather-beaten picket fences frame dead lawns. Above one front porch a striped awning hangs in tatters from a metal frame, snapping in the wind. Here and there the mummified remains of ferns droop over the edges of ceramic pots, and wicker chairs lie on their sides, askew, resting where the careless wind left them.

Stopping in the middle of the street, you cup your hands to your mouth and yell: "Where IS everybody?"

No reply. Just dry leaves scraping across the cobblestones.

"Come on, where IS everybody? Is this some kind of sick joke?"

But no one is laughing …

It is then that a grisly thought chills your spine: *did a nuclear disaster happen here? Did a reactor melt down and poison the area for miles around?*

If so, then you're doomed. It's only a matter of time before your skin starts rotting off your bones. But when you were up by the lighthouse, on that high windy promontory, you didn't spot any telltale cooling towers punctuating the landscape. Of course, it's dark all the time here and if a reactor *had* melted down there might not be any towers left to see. Horrendous thought, but it *would* explain why the town is deserted.

Or did a bomb go off near here?

No, that's not likely … things here don't look destroyed, just old.

Did a plague sweep down the coast … something like a modern version of the Black Death?

Possibly … but if it did, then you must be immune. That would be one good outcome at least.

But more precisely, you feel like a blind person who fell off a cliff—a cliff carved out of Time.

And if that's true, then it may be quite impossible to learn what's really going on here.

It would help to have a car …

For if you had a car, you could leave this town and discover what lies beyond it. But the streets here are as vacant as the houses … not a single vehicle in sight. No car, no truck, not even a horse-drawn carriage or a bicycle. Just grains of sand, swirling in taffeta patterns over the streets …

Near the center of town you come across a small village green where people long ago strolled on Sunday afternoons, maybe listening to John Philip Sousa marches trumpeted from a band shell draped in red-white-and-blue bunting. Today all that remains of those sun-dappled afternoons is the sagging band shell and a small wood-frame church facing a patch of dry grass.

The bushes surrounding the church died during the endless night, their green tendril circuits now desiccated and brown. A bell still hangs in its leaning steeple, however. You may have heard it the other night when you were lying awake in your bed and a powerful wind gusted over the waves. It sounded like the silvery chime of a distant buoy.

The front door stands wide open, as though inviting you in. Entering the shadowy interior, you call out to see if anyone is still here, but the echo of your voice is the sole reply: no pigeons cooing in the rafters, no furtive rat feet scurrying across the floorboards. For a moment your hope of finding people swells when you spot hymnals lying open in the pews. But when you pick one up, the binding disintegrates in your hand, releasing several pages to drift to the floor like autumn leaves.

It's clear that no one has been here for a very long time. The people who held these books probably sang until their hymns turned to death rattles.

The street you have been following terminates at the marshy edge of a channel of water. On the other side, a wide expanse of pampas grass and rushes extends to a misty horizon. Apparently this is a barrier island. So much for heading inland.

Back at the hotel, the first thing you do is to check the guestbook again. But no one has responded to the message you left there. And the mysterious fire is still flickering away in the hearth, apparently untended.

•   •   •

That night, a Technicolor dream illuminates your head. In this dream you're driving a car over verdant hills undulating under the sapphire dome of the sky. The sun flares over fields of golden wildflowers as they release their lascivious perfume into the lush air, and the sunlight feels deliciously warm on your skin. You feel good—light-hearted, exhilarated, the wind filling your sails …

In this high-resolution dream you soon arrive at a bridge made of stone. Some ancient-looking people dressed in rags are gathering under the arches of this bridge. Their leathery faces are lined with age, and cataracts have turned the corneas of their eyes milky-white. They appear to be blind, and yet they are motioning for you to follow them.

Follow them? Where? Even though they're blind, is there a chance they could show you the way out of here?

But just as you are about to join them, you snap back to your hotel room, awake and sweating on your bed, your heart hammering away inside your ribs.

That didn't exactly feel like a dream. Dreams are chaotic, illogical … this vision possessed a narrative, a story …

7

STILL NO EVIDENCE OF A SHIPWRECK HAS APPEARED ON THE BEACH: NO splintered shards of hull or keel, no dented gasoline tanks, no orange life vests bobbing in the surf. There's nothing outside but wind and endless waves. So by now it's become pretty clear: *you weren't shipwrecked, not unless the ship was invisible.*

It's time to try escape route number two: up the coast …

A fresh ocean breeze is circulating through the streets today, wandering in from the flat expanse where there are no borders, no claims or deeds, no human fingerprints. And the air is definitely turning colder. This world may not revolve around a sun, but apparently the seasons here do change.

Is it possible that the Earth spun out of its orbit and is now hurtling through space? No, that can't be … if that were the case, the Earth would be a gigantic ball of ice.

A few small buildings nestle among the wind-blown dunes a short distance up the beach. Most of these structures were painted white a long time ago, although on a few of them flakes of pink and blue enamel still cling to rough gray boards.

The sign on the first building reads: CROWS NEST SALOON. Its interior is dark and cobwebs tickle your face as you step through the swinging doors. A couple of barstools lie overturned in the sawdust covering the floor and a round table with a kerosene lamp on it occupies one corner. Framed sepia photos, mostly of men in bowler hats and handlebar mustaches, fill one wall and a brass spittoon stands on the floor at one end of the bar. Rows of dusty bottles line the shelves. With their monochrome labels and cork stoppers, they resemble old medicine bottles, but they are empty now, their contents having evaporated long ago. There's no sign of food here either — no cartons of biscuits, no tins of sardines, no barrels of dried-up gherkins. It's strange that you feel no thirst here ... no desire to drink anything, alcoholic or otherwise. Not even water.

About fifty yards beyond the saloon, a larger building opens onto a wooden boardwalk — a spacious pavilion with two ornate gaslights flanking its entrance. It must have been an amusement pier, for a painted clown face — now faded to ghostly shades of white and pink — grins above the entrance. Fastened to the wall, a wind-tattered poster announces: PROFESSOR ARBUTHNOT'S AMAZING MAGIC LANTERN SHOW. The illustration depicts a mustachioed man wearing a top hat, standing in front of a wooden box with a lens protruding from it, projecting the image of an Egyptian pyramid onto a screen.

A large carousel dominates the floor inside the pavilion, its red and gold horses frozen midstride. The sight of this extravagant amusement ride conjures up a luminous memory that feels very old — the memory of a sun-drenched summer long ago. Compared to this memory, the dark scene outside looks like a photographic negative — black sky, white sand.

And that impression reminds you of a novel thought you had a little while ago, when you wondered if the Universe has more than one side. What if it's simply a matter of polarities? What if you fell into a coexisting negative side of the positive world? After all, that sort of polarity wouldn't be unique in the universe. We already have a number of polar opposites that define each other: light and dark, outside and inside, good and evil …

And if that's true, then what feels like memories may actually be impressions printed through from the positive world. Maybe the girl you saw in the hotel isn't even a ghost. Maybe she's more like an eidolon — the projected spirit-image of a living person.

Intrigued by this notion, you concentrate on the image of the beach that just illuminated your mind. With eyes tightly closed now, you experience an epiphany so vivid it makes you gasp: this town — this deserted place of empty rooms and dead gardens — was once an amphitheater of joy where warm sunlight was a soothing balm for the sting of winter cold … a place where people sought temporary relief from the tedium of their lives … where they climbed out of their gray suits and corsets, eyes full of light, and yielded just a bit to the sacrilegious appetites of the flesh. Little children, reveling in their new bodies, shrieked with glee as they splashed in the surf and young women anointed their arms with seductive oils of coconut and jasmine. Lovers made vows under the Moon and old people sat on deck chairs, gazing at infinity.

But even as you try to cling to this bright vision, the curtain falls and the theater of your mind is once again plunged into darkness. When you open your eyes, you're heartbroken to find yourself still imprisoned within the same old negative night.

Don't some people say there are pro's and con's to everything?

Your instinctive reaction is to laugh at that notion, but maybe there's something to it: *Why fret so much about memory loss? Why stay mired in the Past? Just get used to being new and move forward … get on with it …*

These words sound reasonable enough, but every fiber of your being rebels at the thought.

A fortune-telling machine stands by the entrance—a polychrome wooden bust mounted behind a glass window in a wooden cabinet. The figure is a grotesque simulacrum of an old woman: white teeth carved in a broad rictus, bulbous eyes, and a violet turban crowning the head. Letters painted on the wooden panel below the window read: MADAME ZIMA SEES ALL, KNOWS ALL. A brass lever protrudes from the side of the cabinet and casually, almost absent-mindedly, you pull on it. Gears grind inside the box. Then the grinning head of Madame Zima nods jerkily and a slip of paper pops out of a slot in the front of the machine. You pull it out and read it:

TELLING THE TRUTH SHALL SET YOU FREE.

BUT IF YOU LIE, FREE SHALL YOU NEVER BE.

You stare at the piece of paper in your hand and frown.

What? Telling the truth shall set you free?

You mull over her prophesy for a minute.

"But," you finally say out loud, "it seems to me that no one can ever be *totally* free. There are always limitations, aren't there? Always shackles and chains—most of them invisible. There you have it … I've told the truth."

You yank on the lever again and another slip of paper pops out. This one reads:

CONGRATULATIONS!
YOU SPOKE THE TRUTH
NOW YOU SHALL BE FREE

"Really? Wait a minute … how can I be free if the truth I told was that no one can ever be free?"

You pull the lever again. Madame Zima nods and another note pops out:

IN TIME ALL SHALL BE REVEALED

When you yank on the lever again, no new response appears. Apparently, Madame Zima has told you all she is willing to reveal for now. You crumple up the slips of paper, throw them onto the floor, and stomp out of the pavilion.

Another building fronts onto the boardwalk not far from the amusement pier. It is a simple wooden shop with large windows and a black shingle roof. A painted sign hangs above the open door:

OLIVIA'S OLDE CURIOSITY SHOPPE
SOUVENIRS AND SUNDRIES

The antique words on the sign sound ironic, since a tiny scrap of memory reminds you that the word "souvenir" means "memory" in some other language.

An open window in the back of the store allows the saline fragrance of the ocean to blend with the attic smell of old wood. For the most part the shelves are bare, but a few items have survived from a previous era: souvenir thimbles, tiny sailing ships inside bottles, partially deflated plastic balls decorated with polka dots, clam shells painted with miniature seascapes, and a yellowed lithograph of the Captain's Quay Hotel with a horse and carriage passing by in front of it.

A metal rack leans on its base just inside the doorway, displaying a single postcard—an old photograph of a Victorian town by the sea, apparently hand-painted. The letters GREETINGS FROM WAVESEND appear on a banner drawn at the top of the card. These letters are printed very close together. It could read WAVES END but on the other hand it could also read: WAVE SEND (although that wouldn't make sense, would it?) *Is "Waves End" the name of this town?* Not clear, but at any rate it fits, so you decide to call it that from now on. The card crumbles in your hand like a sheet of ancient papyrus, the pieces settling on the floor like pieces of a jigsaw puzzle. Apparently this strange town has nothing to offer but disappointment.

Standing there for a moment, looking down at the puzzle-fragments of the postcard, a new inspiration galvanizes you: *wouldn't it be great if you could send a postcard—a sort of message in a bottle—to someone on the Outside? But to whom? And how would that work anyway? Is there maybe a postage stamp in this store that could do that? Well, why not? Nothing else makes much sense here.*

But the drawers below the counters are empty, nothing in them but grains of sand. An ornate metal cash register occupies a table in the center of the floor, but its drawer is also empty. No money, no miraculous stamps …

A little toy spyglass lies on a table near the cash register. The tube is made of faded blue cardboard with pale yellow stars on it. Taking it out to the small deck behind the shop, you raise one end of it to your right eye, pointing the other end of it at the horizon.

A bewildering array of fractal patterns immediately twists in front of your eyes—staggeringly complex self-referencing pinwheels of dots spraying off other spinning pinwheels. For some reason this terrifies you. Reflexively, you fling the spyglass into the waves, where it disappears below the shifting surface with a tiny *ker-plunk*.

Retreating from the edge of the deck, you collapse on a bench, unsettled and confused.

What kind of infernal lens was in that thing?

Once you calm down a bit, you push yourself off the bench and continue your expedition, coming across a few more stores half-buried among the dunes. One bears a sign depicting a bicycle and reading: VELOCIPEDES. Another shop identifies itself with a large sign reading: HABERDASHERY, decorated with the faded images of violets. But all their windows are dark, and when you peer though the smeared glass you see nothing but dust and dead flies and wisps of sand on the floors. There's no getting away from it: Waves End is a dead, forgotten place.

Ocean Avenue continues on its lonely way through the wayward dunes beyond the last shop, eventually leading to a bridge. Even though a thick fog is drifting in, a larger body of land is still visible beyond the concrete span, which looks like it connects this barrier island to the mainland, arching over a narrow stream whose water is sliding serenely into the ocean. The fog also smudges the serpentine road beyond the bridge. That fog sometimes blankets a seaside town is perfectly natural, of course, but this particular fog doesn't look quite right; the images appearing inside it look more distorted than foggy. And the edge of the fog is very distinct, not fuzzy. It looks more like a gray wall.

The wall billows, undulating in front of you.

A little voice inside you warns you to be careful. Cautiously, you pick up a three-foot piece of driftwood lying by the side of the road and toss it into the fog. The driftwood warps instantly, its smooth straight form becoming grotesquely misshapen as it spins through the gray blur and clatters on the road.

For a second, the shock of this spectacle fills you with an unnamable dread.

After taking a few stumbling steps backward, you turn around and run back to the hotel, which now beckons like a tranquil island in the middle of a roiling sea.

It is a huge relief to find the hotel exactly the same as when you left it, including the guestbook, in which no new writing has materialized.

Turning away from the reception desk, however, you stop in your tracks. The girl you saw before is now staring at you from inside the mirror hanging on the far wall, as though she were gazing at you through a window. Her image can't be a reflection, for there's no one besides you in the lobby.

"Hello," you say hesitantly. "Please stay … I want to talk with you."

You take a few steps toward the mirror.

"Do you live here? In this town?"

Her response chimes inside your head, her voice sounding sing-song, as though taunting you: *I know who you are … do you know who I am?*

This revelation makes your heart skip a beat.

"No, I don't know who you are. Who am I? Tell me … please!"

She grins.

Tag, you're it!

Immediately after this outburst, her image dissolves into vertical stripes and then disappears altogether. The sheet of silvered glass framed on the wall turns from window back to mirror, once again reflecting nothing more unusual than the dusty lobby.

You decide to name this playful girl-ghost "Ondine" after the watersprite in ancient mythology. It's as good a name as any for a girl in this watery place.

Before you leave the lobby, you pick up the pen and write in the guestbook:

> Having a wonderful time in Waves End
> Let's get together soon and do something fun!

.   .   .

That night, an incandescent dream transports you to yet another time and place. In this latest vision you're a child, sitting on the front steps of an old cottage, facing an emerald lawn and the placid water of a small lake. You raise a little plastic ring to your mouth and blow a soap bubble. It wobbles in the air for a while, the Earth's new little glassy moon. For a few seconds, a reflection of your face shimmers on its surface. As the bubble throbs, your reflection warps through shades of magenta and gold and then the bubble finally pops, leaving behind a misty rainbow.

The dream leaves behind a warm comfortable feeling that lingers for several minutes after you awaken, but the golden light that sparkled so beautifully on the bubble eventually fades.

Was that also a dream? Or was it a memory … another piece of the puzzle?

8

ment—cryptic and aloof, providing no direction. Whatever promise it holds remains a secret, locked up inside its large many-faceted lens.

The first two escape routes—heading inland and up the coast—didn't work out very well, but there's one more option: heading south—*down* this mysterious coast.

And if you find a boat you may even be able to leave by sea. If you can figure out how to use the sextant in your room, you could set out across the ocean and discover what lies beyond the horizon. Maybe the ruins of your previous life are still out there on some island, waiting for you to return. This is a seaside town after all … there must be a boat somewhere!

You decide to search for one.

Inexplicably, the veranda has become a firefly graveyard. Dozens of them now lie scattered across the weathered boards. Greenish-yellow light still pulses in a few even though they now lie immobile, grounded, their wings motionless. Their flashing seems to follow a regular sequence. Could this be a message? Some kind of code? Maybe a dying wish? If so, to whom?

One more puzzle within an enigma …

Stepping around the glimmering fireflies, you cross the yard to Ocean Avenue and head south. This new day feels strangely flat. The ocean has calmed down, the foaming breakers now slow and gentle. The sky is crystal clear, but as always it is dark. The silver orb of the Moon is nowhere to be seen. Of course, there's no sunlight for it to reflect, so maybe it's out there somewhere but just not visible … a shadow, a total eclipse.

The lighthouse promontory provides a commanding view of the coastline, and the air at this elevation has a bracing briny fragrance, redolent of waving kelp forests and vast shoals of mussels. To the south, a small crescent beach wraps around the base of another rocky bluff sheltering a secluded cove, and in the middle of that cove a rotting pier juts into the water beside a gray wood frame building.

But it's not exactly an idyllic landscape …

A syrupy-looking fog surrounds this cove, smudging the western pine-covered horizon as well as the ocean to the east. This fog looks exactly like the terrifying fog that swallowed up the bridge at the other end of the island—the one that did terrible things to the piece of driftwood that you tossed into it. And unless your mind is playing tricks on you, this fog is creeping closer.

However, when it momentarily recedes from the cove, it reveals a fishing boat lashed to the pier.

A boat! You may have just found your ticket out of here!

You scramble down the rocks and run toward it.

But disillusionment sets in as soon as you approach the sagging pier. The utilitarian wooden building beside it apparently served a commercial fishing fleet at one time, but like the rest of the town it looks abandoned now. The shingled roof must have caved in years ago and many of the boards on the sides of the structure are missing, giving it a skeletal look.

The spindly gangplank connecting the beach to the pier is slippery and some of the planks bend precariously under your feet. White fish skeletons on the slick wood resemble fossils, and the pungent smell of decaying seaweed makes your nostrils tingle.

The building appears to have been a ship chandlery. Inside its ruined walls a few coils of rope lie on the floor next to a pile of fishnet, and corroded eye bolts and turnbuckles occupy a worm-eaten counter.

The boat next to it turns out to be a rusty old scow with nets still draped from the booms above its deck. In the inky water below the pier, schools of fish with silvery zero-eyes sway passively in an invisible current, and below them a few vigilant octopuses lie sprawled on the sand as though waiting for something to happen.

The boat is listing slightly, low in the water, and a gaping hole below the water line informs you that the boat is essentially sunken, its keel resting on the sand. Your hope of escaping by sea vaporizes in an instant.

Feeling thoroughly bleak now, you walk to the end of the pier and gaze into the distance. No ships' lanterns glow on the razor-sharp border between the blackness above and the blackness below. No boats are coming home. All sailors are lost.

The beach south of the fishing pier is a long expanse of dark gray sand littered with hieroglyphic whale bones. As you walk along, another dock materializes out of the fog — a short one with a small boat tethered to it.

And unlike the fishing boat, this boat looks new …

It turns out to be a modern thirty-foot powerboat with an inboard engine. The hull and deck are made of teak, varnished to a glassy finish and decorated with brass fittings in the shape of the Roman god Neptune. Excited, you quickly untie the rope securing it to the dock and climb into it, sitting behind the wheel.

Let's see … it shouldn't be hard to start …

But just as you reach for the ignition, the engine rumbles to life, churning the water behind the boat. Seconds later, the boat pulls away from the dock and heads out to the open ocean, the steering wheel turning by itself.

Leaving land behind makes you feel uneasy at first, but the discomfort soon passes, replaced by intense curiosity: *where is this boat taking you? Could this be your escape?*

The robotic boat buzzes across the dark water for what you estimate is an hour. Waves thump against its keel as it flies over the surface. Above you, one star shines much more brightly than the others—an intense blue-white beacon in the heavens. It looks like the boat is heading in its direction, which appears to be due East.

Soon the water becomes smoother. It feels pleasant, cruising under the stars. A gentle wind is blowing from the horizon, caressing your face. The hum of the boat's engine is the only sound you hear.

Before long, the ocean changes again. The water becomes so still and glassy it looks like a dark mirror, and the engine shuts off with a shudder. The boat slowly glides to a complete stop, and then floats motionless under the sapphire pole star.

An indeterminate amount of time passes, but the boat still doesn't move. It is eerily quiet. Not even the screel of a seagull ripples through the air.

Eventually a few objects drift into view from the horizon: fragments of a life preserver, rotten timbers from a boat's hull, glass floats from fishnets, some plastic bottles, dead fish with shiny white bellies …

This appears to be some sort of sad Sargasso Sea, where the flotsam and jetsam of the world come to their final rest. And now *you* have come here. What does that mean? Have you reached the end of your journey?

You now bitterly regret your decision to climb into this boat. In fact, you fervently wish you were back in the hotel, sitting comfortably in the lobby, watching the eternal fire.

Then, inexplicably, the boat's engine rumbles back to life, its propellers once again churning the water behind the stern. Slowly, the boat inches forward and then sweeps around in a wide arc, apparently turning back toward land.

As the speedboat skims over the gathering waves, a feeling of great relief washes over you. You were not yet ready for that Sargasso Sea. When the motorboat reaches its dock, the engine shuts off by itself. The voyage is over.

It doesn't take long to walk back to the derelict pier with the fishing boat—the sagging dock in the forgotten cove where seabirds circle over their own reflections and the only sound is the slapping of the incoming tide against mossy pilings.

•   •   •

The guestbook In the hotel lobby delivers no new message from the mysterious Ryder. *Why the hell doesn't he or she respond? This is crazy!* And who is the girl, if not Ryder? Why does she keep disappearing? Is she teasing you? Or maybe it's simply hard to connect with you, as though some sort of invisible wall separates the two of you.

Exhausted, you immediately retreat to your room, where you collapse on the bed and sink into a green, watery slumber. In no time at all you're dreaming about mischievous mermaids with moonlight in their eyes and seaweed hair billowing under the waves. They live in sunken ships with sea chests full of pearls and lost compasses, and their outstretched green arms beckon to you, inviting you to join them. For a moment you think you hear them singing to you, but then you spot a pod of Humpback Whales behind them, crooning their otherworldly songs as they flex their tales and propel themselves through the emerald depths. What incredible thoughts might be lighting up those huge brains of theirs? If only you could talk to them.

They probably know a way out of here …

9

 in front of the hotel. It seems that during the night the ocean disgorged hundreds of medusa jellyfish that now lie stranded on the sand. Beyond the breakers many others bob up and down on the shifting field of water. In some of them, phosphorescent plankton glows greenish-yellow, creating the surreal impression that a large shipment of light bulbs just floated to the surface from a sunken freighter.

Curious, you slide down a dune that drifted over Ocean Avenue during the night and approach them for a closer look. Inside their transparent helmets glisten gelatinous *mesogleas* and dozens of wavy tendrils, some of them pink and gold like filaments of Venetian glass. You touch the side of your foot to the umbrella-shaped cap on one of them, carefully avoiding the tentacles bristling with stinging cells. It doesn't move. You try several others. All of them appear to be dead.

The churning breakers deliver even more of the hapless organisms, depositing them on the glossy sand. After spending a few minutes in this jellyfish cemetery, you return dispirited to the hotel.

From the perspective of the veranda, the dead medusas create a grisly tableau: their bulbous bodies and trunks of twisted tentacles look like human brains with spinal cords attached, dissected and displayed on the sand like laboratory specimens.

.   .   .

The next morning, they are gone. Once again, the beach is a blank sheet of sand. The same fathomless ocean that previously ejected you has evidently reclaimed them, for reasons you can't begin to understand.

10

THE BONE-FILLED EARTH UNDER FESTIVE STARS HAS BECOME A STARK emblem of your own mortality: *clockwise through Eternity—curse of the Earth-born.* And during this particular arc of eternity, a chilling premonition has been creeping up on you like a shadow gliding across the ocean floor: it is the suspicion that you'll be marooned here forever. The way home is not likely to be a simple heading, and studying the nautical chart in your room turned out to be a total waste of time; you still have no idea where in the world the coastline depicted on it is supposed to be. The map is mocking you.

No! There MUST be a way out of here … if only you'd find a car somewhere …

Back in the lobby, no new message has appeared in the guestbook. Both Ryder and Ondine are being infuriatingly coy.

However, something new has just materialized in front of the hotel. A car is now parked on Ocean Avenue, and this latest Waves End phenomenon has an odd, premeditated quality.

Is it possible that you wished this car into existence? Material-ized an idea? Could this vehicle be made from mind-infused matter?

Cautiously, you descend the stairs and cross the yard for a closer look.

You don't know anything about cars, but this one looks special. A monumental chrome grill accents the front with big round headlamps flanking it. The sleek body is painted glossy black, and a white-walled tire sits above the right front fender. You circle it a few times, finding a name emblazoned above the grill:

DUESENBERG

That name sounds familiar … this is an old car, isn't it? Is Time actually sliding backward? If so, that could be a good thing, right?. Without even trying, you may yet wind up back where you were before this nightmare began …

You walk around this extravagant automobile a few more times, examining it. *Did someone else arrive during the night and join the mysterious Ryder?* There's no sign of tire tracks on the street — no telltale tread marks in the powdery sand, and the windows in the hotel are still as dark as they always have been. Plus: if someone had pulled up in this big machine during the night, surely you would have heard it. The driver's side door swings open when you pull on the handle, and a key is lying on the driver's seat like an invitation.

You pick up the key, slide across the seat behind the steering wheel, and study the instruments arrayed on the dashboard. Three of the gauges are labeled "Oil", "Brake", and "Revolutions per minute" and there's also a speedometer. You remember that the slotted ignition device in the dashboard is basically a metal jigsaw puzzle and the key is the missing piece.

Of course … you have to insert the key into the ignition and turn it. When you do this, the engine coughs and the needles twitch inside the gauges.

Really … now that's promising! It's incredible that the Jurassic sunlight trapped in swamp grass and dinosaur blood—refined to explosive purity—didn't evaporate ages ago. But against all odds some fuel apparently remains in the tank.

You step on a large foot pedal on the floor and turn the key again. More noise but still no forward motion. You try several more of the ancient devices on the dashboard. When you pull on one knob the engine shakes and then begins a throaty susurration under the hood … *YES!*

Gently depressing the accelerator while you depress another pedal makes the car buck forward a few inches. When you stomp on the brake it stops. The fuel gauge reads half-full.

My God … this is going to work! You're actually going to escape!

Grasping the steering wheel tightly, you feed the engine a little more gas. The car bolts forward again. After a few more of these clumsy lurches, you become accustomed to the friction point of the clutch and the flexibility of the gas pedal. With the engine now humming smoothly, you steer away from the hotel and head up Ocean Avenue toward the bridge at the edge of town.

This time no sinister fog blurs the landscape in front of you. The bridge and the road beyond it look crystal clear—sharp and distinct. *Thank God!* However, the piece of driftwood that twisted so grotesquely in the fog is still lying on the macadam, like a road sign warning of trouble ahead. But rolling over the bridge, you safely leave the oneiric landscape of Waves End in the rearview mirror. An invigorating breeze is sweeping over the whitecaps now. It smells like wide-open space and freedom. You can't help laughing out of pure exhilaration.

Do you dare hope to see a modern city again? An ordinary city of shops and apartment buildings and restaurants, where real flesh-and-blood people go to office buildings and stores?

This tempting visualization becomes your new compass heading.

Ocean Avenue soon becomes a ribbon of asphalt winding through wetlands thick with tall brown grass. The coastline has become wilder and increasingly complex. Instead of smooth sand neatly partitioned by rocky jetties, this new stretch consists of many small inlets, inlets within inlets, tiny bays, and countless notches in serpentine layers of rock.

It is eerily silent, too. No circling seagulls screel in the dead air. It is just you, this phantom car, and the road.

Minutes later, a few single-story buildings appear around a curve. The first of these structures is a dilapidated motel with a row of dark windows and open doors. A sign by the road announces: DRIVE ON INN. This small motel looks like it belongs to a much later period than Waves End, as though this stretch of coast doesn't stick as far into the Past as the town does.

Is it possible that this car came to transport you to a future time?

Whatever year it is, however, the scene is a portrait of utter desolation; there's no evidence of recent habitation ... no cars parked in front, no people inside. The Drive On Inn was clearly abandoned long ago.

Another motel appears a little farther on—this one painted pastel blue. A sad-looking fountain, choked with sand, stands in front of it, and the sign above the office reads: TIKI MOTEL. A fake palm tree and a wooden Tiki statue flank the doorway to the office. This squalid hostelry looks like it came from the same era as Drive On Inn, and it also appears to be deserted.

Out of curiosity, you pull off the road and park in front of the motel office, leaving the engine running since you don't want to take the chance that it won't start again. Inside the office the skeletal remains of a philodendron droop by the door. Dusty Venetian blinds, many of their slats missing, hang crookedly in the window and a guest book lies beside a clamshell ashtray on the counter. Next to the guestbook stands an old black telephone with a rotary dial.

A phone!

It's the first one you've seen since you woke up here.

You quickly grab the handset and hold it up to your ear, but instead of a dial tone, all you hear is a whisper, like the sound of surf.

Pressing the buttons in the handset cradle does nothing, and dialing "O" doesn't even produce a clicking sound. The only sound coming out of the machine is *shh … shh …* like the sound of waves collapsing on a beach. It's as though you were holding a seashell to your ear.

The guestbook also disappoints; every page is blank. If people checked in here recently, they must have been ghosts.

Then a new sound outside catches your attention. The car's engine sounds different. And for good reason: the Duesenberg has vanished. A streamlined bottle-green car has taken its place. Stunned and apprehensive, you walk over to it and examine its sleek body. Chrome letters read: HUDSON HORNET.

Is Time playing tricks on you again?

At least the engine is running. That's reassuring at least …

When you depress the gas pedal the car lurches forward and soon you're back on the road winding through the wetlands.

The next building down the road is a tiny shingled structure whose sign—now hanging precariously by one corner—reads: SEAFOOD SHANTY. A painted cartoon crab, grinning dementedly and waving its claws in the air, fills one side of this sign. Years of sun and rain have faded it to a pale shade of pink, almost bone-white. All the buildings you've seen so far look really old and badly in need of repair.

The narrow road winds through more and more wetland, where a silvery mist floats over rushes and tall grass. A few abandoned cars, rusted to a deep shade of orange, stand by the side of the road and before long hard-packed sand replaces the asphalt under your wheels and you leave the derelict motels and restaurants behind.

The deterioration of the road is a concern, for you have no idea where it will take you and there is no map in the car. It would be very easy to get lost out here. With a shiver you remember how the piece of driftwood twisted grotesquely when you threw it into the fog bank.

Will the monster fog return soon and trap you here, far from the haven of the Captain's Quay Hotel?

Minutes roll by, then hours, or at least that's what it feels like. More buildings appear ahead. You slow down as you approach the first one. It is small building, covered with gray shingles. And it looks familiar.

It is an abandoned restaurant. A sign hanging on it, depicting the cartoon image of a crab, reads: SEAFOOD SHANTY.

Could there be two of these places? Maybe a chain of them?

You step firmly on the gas pedal. Pebbles clatter under the wheels.

Soon another abandoned motel appears by the side of the road. Its sign announces: TIKI MOTEL. Here, you slam on the brakes and screech to a stop. There's no denying it: this is the same Tiki Motel you saw just a little while ago, with the same sand-filled fountain, the same weeds pushing through cracks in the macadam, the same Tiki statue standing guard beside the office door.

Somehow you returned. But how could that be? The road didn't curve around, and you're positive you didn't turn or veer off the highway onto another road.

Warily, you roll forward toward the next structure: the Drive On Inn—the same Drive On Inn that you saw earlier. This car and this road have somehow taken you in an impossible loop.

A few hundred yards beyond the Drive On Inn, the bridge back to Waves End arches over the inlet that you crossed not long ago. Your malaise deepens when you spot dense fog coiling beneath it. Instinctively, you slam your foot on the gas pedal and shoot up the ramp leading to the bridge. You practically fly over it, racing back toward the cobblestone streets of Waves End.

Apparently someone—or something—does not want you to leave.

11

THE NEXT MORNING THE HORNET IS GONE, VANISHED INTO THIN AIR. Not even tire tracks remain in the sand where it stood not long ago. That's not really surprising, though; things come and go here. That's just the way it is. Nevertheless, even though you've become somewhat inured to life in this insane place, your Möbius-loop journey through the wetlands shook you deeply.

Out of desperation a bold new plan crystallizes in your mind. Why didn't you think of it before?

In the room next to yours you pick up the small wooden chair by the bed, and the other rooms provide more firewood. Soon a creaky twenty-foot-high chair pyramid towers above the sand. Snapping a leg off one of them, you return to the lobby, where you shove it into the eternal flames in the fireplace until the end of it catches fire.

Out on the beach, the plume of flame on the end of your torch makes a sound like a flag flapping in the wind, and the dry chairs accept the fire immediately when you touch your torch to the bottom of the pile. One by one they erupt into a vertical cascade of fire, sending sparks spiraling into the sky.

Surely, if someone is out there they'll see this beacon …

The wind blowing off the ocean fans the flames until the chair pile becomes a raging bonfire. The heat feels good. Occasionally you tilt your head and gaze at the sky, hoping to see the lights of a passing plane. But no planes appear … nothing up there but myriad stars set in black infinity …

More time passes … possibly hours …

Eventually the chair-fire gutters out and still no sign of rescuers appears on the horizon. The chairs are gone now. Incoming breakers lick at their ashes.

Back in the lobby, you resume your lonely vigil, hoping against hope that someone in a passing ship saw your signal fire and will soon come to save you.

But another hour passes and still no one shows up. The beach remains a desolate, mystifying place. Resignedly you return to your room and fall asleep listening to the relentless murmur of the surf.

12

The next morning, the miracle-fire in the lobby is still crack-ling away on the hearth. Hoping to see Ondine again, you look for her, but the lobby is still deserted and the mirror on the wall is nothing more than a mundane rectangle of silvery glass. Standing next to the fireplace and gazing at the dancing flames, you hone your courage to a steely resolve: *no no no … you're not going to give up so easily.*

Bounding up the stairs, you collect more chairs from the guest rooms. These you take out to the beach and pile up upon the ashes of your first signal fire. You don't stop until you have collected every chair in the hotel except for the ones in the lobby and the one in your room and stacked them all on top of each other.

This second wooden pyramid turns out to be truly monumental.

It towers above the foaming breakers and, just as you did before, you break a leg off one of the chairs and stick it into the lobby fireplace until it erupts into flame. Holding this torch above your head like an Olympic runner, you race back to the surf and touch the flame to the bottom of the chair pile.

In seconds, the stacked furniture erupts into a blaze that ascends quickly to the apex of the pyramid. Soon the raging fire illuminates the whole beach, flickering on the front of the Captain's Quay Hotel.

Pulling the collar of your shirt tightly around your neck, you scan the inky horizon, summoning the fragile remnants of hope you still carry within you, searching for the lights of a ship. But you know that even if someone on a passing ship happens to see your beacon, they may not send anyone ashore. The water here is certainly too shallow for a large ship to anchor, so the most you can hope for is that someone will report seeing a curious light in this abandoned town and days later a team will come to investigate why people saw a light where no light was supposed to be.

Setting fire to one of the houses along the beach would make a much larger beacon but the wind here can be very strong. There's no telling what might happen if you set an entire building on fire. The blaze could spread quickly and conceivably reduce the entire town to ashes. Then you'd be stuck here without shelter …

Meanwhile, your wooden pyramid has turned into a glorious monument of light, warming the sky, alerting any ship that may be passing in the night.

An hour passes … or so you estimate. But still no ships' lanterns glimmer on the dark water. No Aldis lamps mounted on mastheads signal Morse code for "Hang on, we're coming"… no news at all arrives from beyond the horizon.

Out of loneliness and boredom you start scooping up wet sand and pressing it together next to the crackling blaze. Soon the figure of a person—a sand statue—takes shape under your hands. You slap more wet sand on the figure, making it taller, smoothing it, sculpting the features of a torso, arms, and a face.

When you finish, you stand back and admire your handiwork. It's not bad, actually. But instead of making you feel less lonely, the statue reminds you of just how lonely you really are … how sharply you miss simple human companionship. Above all you miss conversation, the sharing of ideas.

Quietly, discreetly, the tide slides in while the fire slowly transforms the chairs into a mound of ash.

Wait a minute … the Moon causes tides, doesn't it? How did you miss that clue? It's so obvious. But why is the Moon invisible? Where is it hiding?

With a sloshing sound, the cold surf now curls around your statue.

Although your hands created a credible human likeness, you didn't come across any immortality in the sand, so the incoming tide finally swallows up the figure, erasing it from the face of the Earth.

•   •   •

That night, you step into an extraordinarily detailed dream—a hyperdream. This time, you're inside a building—in a large room within this structure. It is a very old building with exposed brick walls, a wood-beamed ceiling, and a floor fashioned from wide rough-hewn planks. It is empty now, but you know that it wasn't always this way. Light dances on the ceiling, a clear indication that the building is located near a body of water. You walk through this dream to a tall window and gaze at a harbor beyond it. Sunlight glares on the still water and the reflections of tall glass-and-steel towers shimmer on its surface. You have the peculiar feeling—not unlike déjà vu—that you were once very familiar with this place even though now you can't even remember where it is.

Did you once live here? Work here?

When you stand close to one of the brick walls, your skin tingles, as though energized by a field of static electricity. This dream — or whatever it is — is so powerful that your heart is hammering in your chest when you awaken.

This couldn't have been a dream … it was too vivid … it must have been another memory — the residue of actual experience …

It seems like more and more of your Past is trickling back through a long-forgotten window in your subconscious mind.

Sitting up on the bed, you close your eyes tight, attempting to use the lantern of your consciousness to see more of the tantalizingly familiar room. For a few seconds, it works. The room reappears, along with the harbor beyond it and the quiet sunlight performing a graceful ballet on the ceiling. You close your eyes tighter and try to make out more details but it's no use. For now, that's it. That is all of the Past that is being revealed to you.

The experience has rekindled your hopes, however. You will file this new high-resolution clue away with the others and more are bound to come. They say patience is a virtue. And after all, this isn't the worst place to be stranded; time moves only within a limited circumference, hunger and thirst aren't problems, and you even have a mystery to occupy your mind through the endless days.

Ah, that is all well and good, but nevertheless you still long to leave … desperate to go home, wherever in the universe home may be.

13

LONG AGO YOU CLIMBED INTO THE PRESENT MOMENT AS THOUGH IT were a lifeboat. That much you remember. It was the only sensible thing to do, since the Past is gone forever and the Future is idle speculation. At least you can *feel* the Present after a fashion, like a current of water passing between your fingers.

But if Time is a river, what is the riverbank?

Is there a way to step out of this endlessly flowing Present onto a timeless shore beside it? And if Time is an infinite series of infinitesimal moments, could one of these moments become a keyhole through which you could glimpse eternity? Maybe by focusing your consciousness into a single dimensionless point of view—a quantum of Time—you could even tunnel your way back to the life you had before you woke up in this nightmare. But how would you do that? It doesn't sound easy, to say the least.

As crazy as it sounds, though, that idea suggests another possible escape route: *through the portal of the mind*. One more time, a wave of stubborn hope crests inside you.

Back in the sanctified stillness of the old cemetery, you try a new approach: you attempt to empty your mind and focus on your lost Past, as though you were holding a spyglass up to your inner eye. You figure that a painstaking and systematic archaeology of memory might just uncover a path leading back to the place you came from.

Okay then … let's try this … focus! What were you doing before you woke up here?

The days, months, and years before your arrival here simply vanished—the way a magician makes an elephant disappear with a wave of his wand. Your amnesia isn't total, however; you obviously remember words and even a few assorted facts—just not the incredibly complex structure of interconnected memories we call "identity". That's too bad, for if you could reconstruct your identity, you might be able to make sense of all this. That could be the key …

But reaching for one's Self is tricky; it's like trying to take hold of one's reflection on the surface of a lake. Touching it makes it break apart and ripple away. It's a fool's errand, like a dog chasing its tail. Nevertheless, the tantalizing sensation of a trace identity lingers inside you, incorporeal as a ghost, challenging you to find it.

You gaze at the blank tombstones surrounding you, as though searching for an answer.

This might be a good time to take stock: what are the clues so far?

Memory loss … trauma? Possibly seeing ghosts … death or a near-death experience? And this mysterious town … that's even tougher to explain. It looks like it belongs to an earlier century. Some sort of time warp then? And your weird ability to see in the dark ... what's that all about? Enhanced mental powers? Possibly resulting from an unusual trauma to the brain, like a blow to the head or a stroke?

Memory *must* have something to do with all this; it's the thread that runs through everything. But it's not like it's a continuous reel of photographic film. Even though a few memories have been trickling back, huge gaps remain. And that's the crux of this enigma.

What caused those gaps? Where *is* the edge of the mind anyway?

It is no doubt the most complicated boundary in the universe. Are we then more complex than isolated globes of encapsulated consciousness? That is, despite all appearances, are we connected in some way? Did the gaps in your memory occur when someone stopped thinking about you?

If we dig deeper and deeper into our own memories, will someone else's memories eventually come to light?

Hmn ... following that line of thought could lead you into a labyrinth from which you'd never emerge.

Okay, forget that. Instead, concentrate on the fundamentals ...

But that's easier said than done, for the more you analyze this mystery, the more the mystery deepens. For starters: we glibly talk about Time and Space, but do we know what those words actually mean?

Time and motion, the fundamental building blocks of perception ... one can't have motion without Time, right? But can one have Time without motion? Time certainly *feels* like it's moving, and it does seem to have a direction. So is a never-ending Time-current carrying us along with it, or are we heroically striding across a geo-temporal landscape from the alluvial plain of the Past toward the still-invisible Future, where Time is bursting out of a crack in Space? Does everything in the Past really vanish into thin air, or do we just march on to another location on the continuum, leaving it behind?

This question lies at the heart of your predicament, for if we effectively choose our path through Time and Space, then we possess some degree of free will. You could simply think: *I will leave this place,* and that thought makes it happen. But if all we do is float along in a swift current, or be blown over the Timescape by some sort of cosmic wind, then we are blithely drifting along with everything else and merely *imagine* that we decide to do what we are doing. We would be nothing more than observers, watching the stage of reality from our ingenious balconies of bone.

Another memory surfaces. No, that's overstating it. It's more like the shadow of a memory, for it's not a discrete image or even a recognizable sound. It is just a vague feeling, but at this point the return of *any* memory is exciting.

It's starting to come back to you: once upon a time you were looking for something … you were desperately searching for something very important … but what was it?

You concentrate really hard on this ember of a memory, as though trying to turn a thought into a thing, for you sense that mental concentration often follows a definite progression: first an inchoate idea, followed by an image … and if you concentrate on that image long enough, it finally becomes so concentrated—so eidetic—that it feels palpable: *real-ized.*

The memory clarifies a bit more …

At some point in the dim Past you felt imprisoned within the invisible walls of language and were desperately searching for something solid—something fundamentally *real*—beneath the latticework of words that stretches to the horizon. It was as though you were trying to reclaim a pristine mind that the prism of the senses hadn't polarized yet … as though you were trying to return to an ancient Elysian Field …

More details coalesce …

Yes, that was it!

Once upon a time you tried to glimpse the world the way it must have looked before human experience became calendared and vocabularized. You tried to lift the linguistic veil and peek beneath it — to gaze upon stark reality, unfiltered by the blurry entanglement of words with all their mind-numbing rules and categories and connotations.

Linguistic proliferation has always been a mixed blessing. Words are such little things, yet we expect so much of them!

And here's another perspective: raw perception — like the wide-eyed perception helpless infants have — could actually be a very dangerous thing: electrifying your brain, frying neurons. In fact, a struggle to purify your vision could have been what transported you here.

Or … maybe your teleportation had more to do with a conversation you once had.

Maybe one day, during an especially intense internal dialog, you talked to yourself, thereby splitting yourself in two, and one of you wound up here as a castaway — either the Speaker-You or the Listener-You. Hard to know which.

In any case, it's clear that you still haven't found what you were searching for.

A chilling conclusion seems inescapable: if life is a box, words don't open it anymore. Far too much grammar has been forgotten.

·　　　　　·　　　　　·

A lurid dream envelops you that night: your lighthouse talisman has finally come back to life, its lens turning into a fiery sword of light sweeping over shoals of uninhabited skulls and dreaming clams. As the brilliant blade spins around, the sky turns inside-out and a swarm of angels arrives, as though summoned by it. They swoop down with their terrifyingly pure faces and key rings jingling at their sides. You are convinced that they can solve your mystery … they know more words than you do …

14

THIS MORNING'S PUZZLE: IF YOU *HAD* SPLIT IN TWO, WHAT WOULD speaker-You look like? How could you tell if what you are now is Speaker-You or Listener-You? How do the antipodal-yet-connected halves differ from each other? Logic suggests that a Speaker knows something, communicates something. You don't speak very much here, but that's because there's no one around to listen, not because you have nothing to say. Listeners would of course listen a lot … they would be very attuned to their surroundings. That certainly describes what you've been doing since you woke up here. You've been more than attentive … you've been downright studious.

But this may be over-thinking things. The phenomenon may not be so clear-cut. Maybe Speaker-You also listens a bit, and Listener-You speaks from time to time. Maybe the two halves of you are simply mirror reflections of each other that function in a similar fashion. It could even be that the appearance of two distinct halves is itself nothing more than an illusion, a way your mind once dealt with loneliness. Or what if the trauma you may have experienced was just the latest division — the latest disintegration—of a larger universal Self? Maybe there's been a long series of these fractures for everyone, going back countless eons … back to an original, primordial rip in the fabric of reality. Have all of us been trying to put things back together ever since?

And could it be that the most recent fracture is what ruptured your memory? What would happen if the two halves—Speaker-You and Listener-You—were rejoined? Would that finally make things right again? Would it make you whole?

It's maddening!

And sadly you realize that you could ponder questions like this for a lifetime and still never find your way home.

·   ·   ·

A new piece of paper has appeared on the front desk, next to the guestbook. It is a crisp piece of fine stationery with the name RYDER embossed in gold at the top. Below that name are penned the words:

SANDPIPER LANE

I HAVE SOMETHING YOU SHOULD SEE

So … it looks like Ryder lives around here and wants to show you something.

This could finally be the break you've been waiting for—

You remember seeing a street named Sandpiper Lane near the old village green and it doesn't take long to reach it. There, another surprise awaits you: a small building that you never noticed before. It's a one-story wooden structure painted white with glossy black trim; the windows are dark, like all the windows in this town. Seashells crunch under your boots as you approach the door for a closer look. Inside its leaning walls is what appears to be a small laboratory. A gentle push on the door makes it squeak open.

"Ryder?" you call out into the gloom. "Are you here?"

No answer.

"Ryder? What do you want to show me?"

Again, no response. You step inside.

The interior consists of one large room with a vaulted ceiling arching over a floor made of small hexagonal black and white ceramic tiles. A brass gaslight assembly hangs from the rafters, a long oak table dominates the center of the floor, and tall bookcases line the walls. The table is loaded with antique laboratory equipment, including a brass microscope, dusty Erlenmeyer flasks, Petri dishes, and specimen jars of varying sizes. Each jar bears a small white label bordered in red but the labels are blank.

The books on the sagging bookshelves are all thick scientific texts published during the nineteenth century. Their leather bindings look brittle and their pages have turned yellow. Most of the titles are in English but a few are in German. A framed collection of butterflies hangs on one wall.

So Ryder is—or was—a scientist. What might he or she have been studying here? Marine biology? What else would you study in a place like this?

Then a picture hanging on one wall catches your attention. It is a crudely-executed image of a lighthouse, sketched in charcoal. It looks like the one perched on the promontory at the edge of town—*your lighthouse, the one that you feel is subtly linked to your presence here.*

Some of the flasks lined up on the table contain a grayish-white granular substance. When you pour some of the contents into the palm of your hand, sparkling granules of quartz, mica, and feldspar sift through your fingers. In other words: sand.

What was Ryder doing with ordinary sand scooped from the beach out front?

A large bottle next to the flasks is empty except for a white film on the bottom—the source of a faint saline fragrance. Apparently the bottle once held ocean water. Ryder must have taken samples of sand and water from the beach. But why? What was this mad scientist looking for?

Ever more curious, you pull the microscope closer to you. The glass slide mounted on its moveable stage looks like it once held a drop of water—a specimen that evaporated long ago, leaving behind a tiny pearl-white smear. You peer through the eyepiece and recoil in horror.

A complex pattern of self-replicating dots wheels in front of your eyes. The pattern is the same as the one you saw when you looked through the toy spyglass at Olivia's Olde Curiosity Shoppe—the one that you re-flexively tossed into the waves.

Could this be what Ryder wanted to show you? Is it possible that these fractal images signify something? Something important?

You push the microscope away.

Did moving beyond your habitual alphabetical thinking take you to a level beneath the surface of things? Has some sort of super-gravity pulled you down to the bare chaotic floor of reality?

There have to be some answers here! Ryder must have kept a research log ... a diary of some sort ...

But the drawers under the table prove to be empty except for the one on the very bottom. It contains a toy spyglass exactly like the one you found in the souvenir shop.

That seems to confirm your earlier suspicion: the wild, twisting images in the spyglass and microscope are important. But what do they mean?

"Ryder?" you yell again. "Hey, are you here? Can you see me? Can you hear me?"

Still no response …

Yet there can no longer be any doubt that Ryder is trying to communicate with you. But a perplexing thought occurs to you: is it possible that "Ryder" is actually Speaker-You … the half of your original identity that happened to stumble upon this laboratory before Listener-You arrived?

15

THE HALL-OF-MIRRORS GAME THAT RYDER IS PLAYING WITH YOU IS GET-
ting old really fast. Why would anyone play a sadistic game like that?
Just to tease you? To torment you? Would Speaker-You actually do this
to Listener-You? Or is it simply that you and Ryder are ghosts trying to
contact each other and not having much success? Can two spirits even *see*
each other? Who knows?

In the lobby, another clue has materialized beside the guestbook: a piece
of paper that wasn't there before. This time it's not a piece of personal stationery; it looks like a sheet from a doctor's prescription pad:

THE STRAND APOTHECARY

SPINNAKER STREET

Rx: TINCTURE OF OPHTHALMA

16

SPINNAKER STREET IS A PICTURESQUE COBBLESTONE CUL-DE-SAC NOT far from the laboratory. Only a few buildings face the narrow lane, including another little wood-frame shop situated in the middle of an overgrown lot. Golden letters on the large front window read simply:

APOTHECARY

You don't remember seeing a drugstore in this town, but here is one, standing right in front of you. It feels solid when you touch it—not at all like a mirage. The front window showcases several dusty bottles in various shapes and sizes, containing red, green, and gold liquids. The largest one, in the shape of an ancient Greek amphora, hangs suspended from the ceiling by two thin brass chains. An alabaster mortar and pestle occupy the center of the space, and behind those items stands a row of bottles containing powders, roots, and shriveled berries. Inside the shop, a white porcelain bust with black lettering on it—the kind once used in phrenology—rests on top of one of the cabinets.

Your reflection in the window startles you. For a second your body doesn't look familiar, as though you borrowed it from someone else. It's tempting to study the reflection, in the hope that it might release more trapped memories, but it makes you feel uneasy. Fortunately the weird disembodied sensation doesn't last long, and when you pull on the handle of the door it swings open.

The air inside the shop is redolent of the Earth, infused with forest-floor fragrances of ferns, mushrooms, and mossy roots. Rows of tiny wooden drawers fill a long cabinet and an array of glass vials stands neatly arranged on a zinc counter. One of these containers looks different from the rest. It is round, about two inches in diameter and is made of opalescent glass. The label reads:

DOCTOR RYDER'S MIRACLE BALM

TINCTURE OF OPHTHALMA

*A Salubrious Balm for Those Afflicted with
a Curious and Restless Spirit.*

This must be what the prescription recommended: *Ophthalma … ophthalmologist*? Sounds like it has something to do with the eyes …

And it looks like Ryder is a doctor, which means that the little girl can't be Ryder. Apparently there are *two* spirits here … maybe three, if you count yourself.

The round glass container is filled to the rim with a white oleaginous cream. This cream has no fragrance, but your skin tingles when you rub it between your fingers. Curious, you put a dab of it on the top of your left hand and rub it into the skin.

No sooner do you finish rubbing it in than your hand disappears.

The jar shatters when it hits the floor. When you try to touch the invisible hand with your right hand, there's nothing there but air.

Hell, your hand isn't invisible ... it's gone!

Terrified, you run out of the shop, bounding over Ocean Avenue to the beach, where you kneel at the water's edge and plunge the arm with the missing hand into the icy surf. Gradually, feeling returns to the empty space where your hand used to be. Then, under the shimmering surface of the seawater, it slowly re-materializes.

When it looks normal again, you pull it out and touch it.

It's solid again! Thank God!

The ocean washed off the Miracle Balm. You clench your hand and flex your fingers. Everything seems to have returned to normal, except for the feeling of raw horror still clawing at your gut. Slumping on the sand, you yell: "*Ryder ... what the hell just happened? Where did my hand go?*"

The surf provides no answer. But as you kneel there on the wet sand, the grinning face of Ondine flickers for a moment in the glassy water.

"Ondine? Did you do this?"

Her image dissolves in the foam of another breaker.

"Ondine! Talk to me!"

But she is gone. Still up to her old tricks ...

•   •   •

Later, lying exhausted on your bed, you reflect on the events of the last few days: the futile trip in the phantom cars, the exchange of cryptic notes at the front desk, and finally Ryder's terrifying balm.

So far, your life here has been insular, introverted, topologically closed. Could Time really be at the bottom of all this? After all, there's this time-warp town, the way things always feel suspended here … and those cars! It's as though you conjured them with your mind!

It's becoming increasingly clear that your mind and this little town, like two sides of the same coin, cannot be separated. Simple logic dictates that Waves End would exist even if you weren't looking at it. But would it be exactly the *same* town? After all, the sages tell us that Seer and Seen cannot be separated; it seems to be impossible to *see* without seeing *something*. The conclusion therefore appears to be inescapable: somehow, in some complex way, you are imbedded in Waves End.

And although you're loath to admit it, it's looking increasingly likely that there's no way out. You are quickly running out of options.

17

A WINDSTORM MUST HAVE BLOWN ACROSS THE BEACH WHILE YOU SLEPT, because roving dunes have claimed even more of Waves End. In fact, so much sand drifted over Ocean Avenue that the street would be impassable now even if another magic car appeared. Up on the promontory, the lighthouse is still dark. If it is projecting anything at all now, it is not projecting light.

Leaning on the railing of the veranda, you still can't push the events of the previous day out of your mind. The memory of how Doctor Ryder's Tincture of Ophthalma made your hand disappear still makes you tremble.

Where did your hand go after you rubbed the balm on it? Did it poke into an alternate universe? What would happen if you apply it to your face, your eyes? Would you be able to peer into that universe? If you slather it on your entire body, would it transport you there? Do you need to disappear here in order to appear somewhere else? As unlikely as it sounds, could Doctor Ryder's Miracle Balm actually be your ticket out of here?

What to do?

You could go back to the apothecary and try the cream again. The jar fell and broke, but the cream is probably still there on the floor.

Using it again would be an extremely dangerous thing to do, of course, but what have you got to lose? Spending the rest of your life in this museum curated by ghosts? Deprived of the simple comfort of sunlight? Trapped in a monadic mind-bend, stretched across the electric boundary between Life and Death?

Long ago, when you were a child, you imagined that your soul might be like a homing pigeon that flies to a distant star at the moment of death. Now, however, you suspect that Hell may actually be eternal life. And, as with many of your thoughts recently, that suspicion inspires yet another puzzle: *we recognize things by their shapes, don't we? If a life is so unimaginably vast that it has no end, then it would have no form, no dimensions as we know them. And if it has no form, would it have any meaning? Could we even perceive it?*

This nagging riddle persists in your mind for some time, like an image burned into your retinas, but no solution surfaces.

Taking a deep breath, you decide to give Ryder's Tincture of Ophthalma another try, come what may. Both terror and hope electrify your nerves as you strike out across the dunes again.

But another shock awaits you on Spinnaker Street. The apothecary shop has vanished — evaporated like a reflection in a dewdrop. Now an empty lot overgrown with nettles and brown grass occupies the place where the shop stood just the previous day. If the apothecary shop was once an open door for you, it is closed now, possibly forever.

A thousand thoughts race through your mind as you stand there in the cold wind whipping off the ocean.

So are all things in this town nothing more than bubbles of sea foam? Or are you just looking at things through an inadequate lens? Maybe the mind is like a prism: you see one thing when you look through it at one angle, and when you turn it you see something else. Maybe that's how it works. Maybe all you need to do is to rotate your mind … but how would one do that? It's probably a long-lost art …

Walking back to the hotel, you decide to analyze the sources of your information, since what we call "reality" could be just the magic lantern show of the senses. First of all, what do you really know about this place? And how do you know it? Most of what you think you know you've learned through your eyes, and intuitively you understand that the pupils of your eyes, like the number zero, are holes through which the Outside comes in. But for you the boundary between Inside and Outside became hopelessly complex. Clearly, you can no longer trust what your eyes are telling you. Maybe you never could. Actually, you feel like you stepped into the space inside a mirror. Some things look the same, but other things look reversed. Instead of mind existing within matter, it feels more like matter exists within mind. Even the direction of Time seems to alternate here. Sometimes it feels like it's moving forward, but at other times you have the giddy feeling that it's sliding backwards.

And you can't help wondering if this negative space you've fallen into has altered your own timeline. Is it possible that being here will enable you to win the ultimate Faustian bargain (*Sure, you can live, but only on one condition: you must eventually die …)*

Does Death exist here? Could this be the one place in the Universe where no one ever dies?

What a thought …

As the Captain's Quay Hotel comes into view, an elegant theory pops into your head. The simplicity of it takes your breath away, for it seems to explain so much: if reality is a sphere (as the universe supposedly is) maybe the flat Cartesian plane of the rational mind cuts crosswise through it, creating a circle where the two forms intersect. Maybe that's why, whenever you try to figure out what happened to you, you go 'round and 'round in circles …

18

WAVES END IS FULL OF SURPRISES. LATER THAT SAME DAY, TINY DOTS OF light begin to sparkle all over the dunes. At first, the source of this light is a mystery, for your talisman lighthouse remains dark; it is not projecting this amazing planetarium display. Overhead, however, the stars are shining more brightly than ever before. In fact, they have become brilliant, nothing short of dazzling. Even stranger: the pattern of lights on the sand exactly matches the constellations above, and you realize that the dots of light you're looking at are actually the pinpoint ends of those very distant stars.

And they're so beautiful!

You bolt through the front door of the hotel and trudge quickly across the dunes to the edge of the surf, where diamond stars fill the entire sky all the way down to the water. It's as though you're standing on a wobbly asteroid suspended in Outer Space, floating weightless among the stars. Of all the mind-blowing surprises this place has presented so far, this is the most incredible.

High above the breakers, one star in particular stands out among the astral archipelagos. It is a pinpoint of painfully bright light—perhaps a supernova. And a strange thing happens when you focus on it: instead of seeing a simple point of light, you see a shifting, shimmering pattern. It is a mesmerizing Lissajous pattern that constantly pulsates and rotates.

Curiously, these pulsations display a definite pattern: every few seconds they shift, rotate, grow larger, collapse, and then repeat. Stranger still: their twitching rhythm seems to be in synch with your heartbeat. Somehow this star is connected to you.

Minutes pass … maybe hours … hard to know, since all sense of time has deserted you. Finally, with a supreme effort, you manage to pull yourself away from this hypnotic spectacle, lowering your eyes to the sand. Carefully keeping your head down, you hurry back to the hotel, where you linger in the lobby for a moment, gazing out the windows at the roiling surf.

That superluminary star was trying to tell you something, but the secret of its ice-cold light remains agonizingly out of reach. Sadly, you couldn't read the code.

19

SHORTLY AFTER THE STAR-SHOW ENDS, THE BIGGEST STORM SO FAR blows in. A gale-force wind sweeps over the waves, churning the water into wisps of spindrift, pushing huge swells that roll across the surface and crash onto the beach. Shutters on the hotel bang loudly in the furious wind, and out on the veranda raindrops sting your face as you slide wooden beams across the windows. While you work at securing the shutters, dozens of blue-white lightning bolts crackle from the bottom of the clouds, apocalyptically arcing down to the heaving whitecaps.

Even more ominously, water has started to spill over the sea wall and spread across Ocean Avenue. This is a very alarming development, for if the water gets too high you'll have to retreat inland, and that's the last thing in the world you want to do. All your instincts warn you that if you leave the coast you will give up all hope of finding your way home.

But remaining here could prove fatal. For all you know, a tsunami could be racing silently toward Waves End at this very moment …

Back in your room, you try hard to stay awake in case the rising water forces you to evacuate. But before long, the wind dies down to a whisper and ocean water stops cascading over the seawall and splashing onto the street. You eventually drift off into sleep, and shortly another dream transports you to yet another strange place.

You dream that you have gone exploring again and have discovered a small airfield north of town where vintage single-engine planes stand on an otherwise deserted runway, their propellers pointed toward the stars. A couple of them are leaning to one side, the tips of their wings touching the tarmac. They look like injured birds, their broken wings condemning them to remain on the Earth.

A small terminal faces the airstrip, its control tower silhouetted against the stars. But its windows are dark: no air traffic controller is inside … no one is managing the heavens here.

One of the planes looks intact. Starlight gleams on its aluminum fuselage, and its wings are straight and its cockpit is open, as though extending an invitation. A ladder mounted on wheels provides a convenient way to climb up to the pilot's seat.

The cockpit feels comfortable, if narrow, and almost immediately the propellers begin to rotate. The engine shudders and belches black smoke.

Ka-chunk … rumble … fwop fwop fwop … whirr ….

The propellers are spinning rapidly now … the plane inches forward …

Wouldn't it be fun if it took off? This could be one last escape route: into the air!

The propellers spin faster and faster and the plane continues to move quickly down the runway. Automatically, flaps on the wings turn downward, and soon you are up in the air, soaring over the airfield. Levers in front of you move by themselves as the plane climbs even higher. The altimeter soon reads 3,000 feet.

It feels like you're flying the plane with your mind. But then again, maybe you're merely a passenger …

From this altitude, Waves End is just a dark maze of streets at the edge of the ocean; the endless breakers are thin white lines far below you. You feel wonderfully, ecstatically free. In fact, it feels like flying is the most natural thing in the world!

Then, the stars begin to separate in front of you … the sky dilates … the plane's propeller spins even faster …

But as the plane approaches this aperture, you abruptly awaken, finding yourself back on the sad old heavy Earth.

It takes a minute to transition to full wakefulness.

That dream felt so real!

It felt like you were actually sitting in that airplane, soaring above the waves like a seabird. Was this intense fantasy triggered by that supernova you saw flaring in the sky? Did the long needle of light from that star trip some switch buried deep inside your brain?

The memory of the airfield and the plane soon fades, leaving behind a residual question: flying in that plane felt like driving those cars up the coast. But you weren't dreaming then … or were you?

Could it be that the difference between Waves End and a dream is merely a matter of density?

20

THE NEXT MORNING, THE STORM HAS MOVED ON AND THE SKY IS CRYSTAL clear again. During the night, the fierce wind swept sand all the way up to the edge of the hotel veranda. A new sand dune now conceals the stairs leading down to the front yard, and Ocean Avenue and the seawall are completely buried. Even more unnerving: the beach in front of the hotel has become a Hieronymus Bosch tableau of dead seagulls. Hundreds of them cover the slate-gray sand, scattered among constellations of starfish. Farther out, white feathers cover the water like a macabre brocade, rising and falling in the swells rolling gently in toward land. The storm must have blown them off course during the night and they no doubt exhausted themselves fighting the wind, dropping from the sky like falling angels. Walking among them, you notice that their glassy eyes are wide open, staring, most of them focused on the countless stars above.

The funereal scene on the beach is unbearably depressing, so you quickly retreat to the tranquil ennui of the hotel, where you sit in the lobby for hours among the wing chairs and dusty tables, still alone, still gazing at the fire that never goes out.

• • •

The memory of the dead gulls weighs on you even after you awaken the next morning, but when you peer out the window you discover that they are all gone — just like the earlier medusas. The sandy terminus in front of the hotel is clear again.

21

A FEW DAYS LATER, YOU AWAKEN TO FIND THAT THE AIR IN YOUR ROOM has turned ice-cold, and outside the window falling crystals fill the sky. Thick flakes of snow are drifting slowly down to earth. Some of them dance in the air for a while, as though weightless, before continuing their descent, and you imagine you hear microscopic tinkling sounds as these hexagonal crystals of ice knock together on their long journey downward. In front of the hotel, Ocean Avenue now slumbers under a pristine white blanket. Snow is falling as far as you can see.

So there can no longer be any doubt about it: the seasons do change here. Waves End just moved from Autumn to Winter.

Taking the sea captain's coat from the cedar chest, you slip it on again, over the other clothes you found.

Strange how all the clothes here fit you …

The snow is so beautiful you linger for a while on the veranda, shivering and gazing up at the heavens. Sparkling snowflakes continue to filter down through the black sky—each one of these crystals unique, no two exactly alike. They gradually descend to the flat gray water in front of you, where they dissolve, returning to the Mother Ocean and disappearing for all time.

Is this another clue? If so, what is the message? A tedious moral fable about the impermanence of all things … about the folly of human vanity?

A much clearer message awaits you on the front desk:

YOU ARE RUNNING OUT OF TIME

Ryder again? Damn it! What kind of twisted game is he or she playing now?

It's far from clear. But whatever the game is, something tells you that you have to play it. You feel like you have no choice.

The top floor of the hotel serves as a useful observation deck, and now as you gaze out the large Palladian window there, an amazing sight takes your breath away: a feeble light is flickering in the window of an old mansion one block from the beach. It's the first light you've seen in any house here.

Now this surely must be a sign!

22

THE HOUSE WITH THE LIGHT IS AN ITALIAN REVIVAL MANSION WITH A large second-floor bay window overlooking a wide lawn. A placard over the front door reads: SUNRISE VILLA and two floor-to-ceiling windows, framed by peeling green shutters, flank the entrance. You've seen the house before but never had a reason to enter it. What rivets your attention now is the golden glow wavering behind the windowpanes.

At last you may come face to face with the elusive Ryder. Or if not Ryder, then maybe Ondine, the mischievous Sprite of Waves End ...

The front door is wide open, but this is not unusual given that most of the doors in this town gape open.

"Ryder?" you holler into the vestibule. "Hey, Ryder? Are you up there?"

No response ...

Oil paintings in ornate frames line the paneled stairwell—portraits, most of them, stern looking Victorian faces peering out through a century of amber varnish. One is a bearded sea captain, wearing a jacket not unlike the one you found in your hotel room. One of Ryder's ancestors? Or maybe Ryder himself?

The wooden stairs squeak as you climb to the second floor, where you find the door to the room with the bay window also standing open.

"Ryder?" you call out again, but again no one replies. Whoever may be waiting for you in the room is playing it very cool.

The dank smell of long-entombed air, laced with the smoky fragrance of oak, hits you in the face when you enter. Logs snap in a large marble fireplace, obviously the source of the light you saw from the hotel window. The architecture of this room is intricate, reflecting a time when labor was cheap and raw materials were plentiful: hand-carved egg-and-dart cornices outline the coffered ceiling and elaborate paneling fills the walls. Carved in deep relief just below the mantelpiece of the fireplace are the words:

TEMPUS FUGIT

Time flies?

That's a really weird thing to engrave on a fireplace. The shutters on the windows are open to the night, providing a wide-angle view of the canted rooftops beyond, but the strangest thing about this room is that it is full of clocks—literally hundreds of them, filling every wall, even the narrow space above the windows. No mirror hangs in the room, however—no silvery surface for Ondine to use as a window.

Exploring this odd shrine to Time, you pull out drawers in the two side tables flanking a leather Chesterfield sofa. There's nothing in them but a few gold pocket watches, the hands on all of them pointing to "12".

An elaborately carved wooden clock towers above the mantelpiece, extending all the way to the ceiling. It looks very old, very European. The figure of a human skeleton, sculpted from ivory, stands on its right side, holding a chain connected to a tiny gold bell. On the left side stands the polychrome figure of a Renaissance philosopher studying a book. Two overlapping brass rings, engraved with numbers and symbols, occupy the space between them. Traditional zodiacal signs fill the outer ring and the inner ring displays strange symbols that you've never seen before.

When you glance at the dial, the hands on the clock suddenly budge.

What just happened? Why did the hands move?

This unexpected development suggests an experiment: you fix your eyes on the zodiacal ring and sure enough the hands move again, this time rotating through several degrees of arc.

Then a tinkling sound jolts you out of your intense concentration. The skeleton on the mantel clock is yanking on the chain connected to the golden bell. Seconds later the gears inside it start grinding away and the clockwork springs back to life. In fact, the hands on every clock in the room have awakened from their slumber, resuming the circular motion that imitates the rotation of the Earth.

Tick-tock-tick-tock-tick-tock …

This is amazing! This is huge! It's the first time you've come across working clocks in this town. Someone—or something—must have wound them up at some point and now they are chattering away, gears whirring, flywheels spinning …

Seconds later, the clocks strike the hour in a glockenspiel chorus of metallic whispers, deep gongs, brassy chimes, tinkling bells, and the warbling of robotic cuckoos. Tiny golden cherubs have awakened and now strike their hammers against miniature bells; Black Forest woodsmen swing their axes at tree-chimes; cuckoo birds poke their heads out of tiny dormer windows; Greek maidens pluck the strings of gilded lyres; a bronze horse caracoles on a golden stage; and on the clock with the skeleton, hooded medieval figures emerge on a rotating disk, with the final figure being the Grim Reaper shouldering his terrible scythe.

Over the deafening chorus of bells you yell: "Hello … is anyone here? Ryder? Are you there? Hello?"

But still no one answers.

Then as chime-echoes fade, the hushed *tick-tock-tick-tock* of the clocks' maniacal counting once again fills the room. Outside, the sky has cleared and this preternaturally motionless seacoast has sprung into motion; constellations of stars are now transiting over Waves End. Or could it be that the Earth has simply resumed its normal rotation? For a moment you imagine that you actually feel the gigantic ball of rock turn under your feet

What is going on here? Has the Earth started to spin out of control?

The sight of the moving stars makes you dizzy. Your knees buckle and you feel like you're about to dissolve—the way you felt not long ago in your hotel room. To steady yourself, you press the palms of your hands firmly against the window frame and mercifully the vertigo soon passes. Then, when you look out the window, you get another shock: a dim amber light is glimmering within the Fresnel lens atop the lighthouse. Your talisman has finally awakened …

As you stare at the wavering light, a novel idea pops into your head: *what if it's not signaling to ships? What if it is signaling to you?*

23

BOUNDING OVER THE SNOW-COVERED DUNES, YOU FEEL WEIGHTLESS, AS though the Earth had lost its gravity. The wind sweeping off the ocean gained considerable momentum while you were in the clock house, and now it feels like it's blowing right through you. At the top of the lighthouse, the large lens is still not rotating, but the glow within it has turned brilliant orange, making it look like a huge topaz crystal. You're shivering, and don't know whether it's because of the cold or because of excitement.

The door of the lighthouse keeper's cottage hangs wide open now, the corroded padlock dangling loosely from its latch. Inside the cottage the whitewashed walls, the oak table, the wooden chair, look no different than they did before: coldly austere — the dwelling of someone who does not care about physical comfort. The place doesn't even appear to have a bedroom, unless it's a tiny chamber higher in the tower. You pull open a drawer in the table, hoping to find a clue, a scrap of history. But it is empty.

At the far end of the room, however, a small wooden door gapes open and behind it a narrow staircase spirals up to the lantern room. Your heart pounds as you run over to it and ascend the dizzying stairs.

Inside the lantern room, you abruptly stop and gasp. A man is lying on a cot at the base of the gleaming lens.

What do you know … it looks like someone else washed ashore …

He looks peaceful, lying there. Not as peaceful as the newly deceased, but peaceful nevertheless … a man at rest. Could *this* person be the elusive Ryder? Is he the lighthouse keeper?

You step closer.

He has a beard and long gray hair, and he's wearing a dark blue suit with shiny brass buttons. It looks like a navy uniform, but not of any navy in this century. He is also wearing boots with sand encrusted on the soles and a large pocket watch hangs from a chain attached to his belt. But the strangest thing is: a helmet-like mask wraps around his head, concealing his face.

"Hello?" you say tentatively, but he doesn't respond.

"Hello?" you repeat politely. "Are you Mister Ryder? I'm sorry, I hate to bother you, but …"

No response. His chest is gently rising and falling, however, so you know he is alive. Probably asleep. You touch his arm, giving him a gentle shove.

"Hey, are you okay?"

Still no response.

"Excuse me … sorry to wake you, but I really need to speak with you. It's important. What did you mean by: 'You are running out of time'? I'm guessing it was you who wrote that in the hotel guestbook—"

When he still doesn't respond, it occurs to you that he could be in a coma. You lean over him and examine the strange mask covering his face. It's like nothing you've ever seen. It consists of a curved piece of glass shaped like the visor of a medieval helmet. The glass is partially silvered, reflecting the image of your face superimposed on the face beneath it. This mask is secured by three leather straps that wrap around the man's head, anchored by a series of brass setscrews. The leather looks like something you'd see on a museum artifact; its surface has begun to crack and flake off. In fact, the lowest of the three straps is broken, a section of it missing. It reminds you of the section of leather strap you found in your hotel room.

A curved strip of highly-polished brass, engraved with a series of symbols, wraps around the top of the visor. These symbols are geometrical rather than alphabetical, as though the device's creator had no words for what the symbols represented. From left to right they increase in complexity from a simple square to intricately nested polygons. Several of the engravings on the brass have been rubbed so smooth they are now barely visible.

Then with a jolt you remember where you saw symbols like these before: the runic symbols engraved on the inner ring of the massive clock in the *Tempus Fugit* house.

So … is the Light Keeper the same person as the Time Keeper?

At that moment, an image wavers in the visor …

A swirling pattern of light glows inside the glass: firefly-green dots pulse and spin, and these mesmerizing dots soon coalesce to form an image. A lake appears. This image has a surprisingly high resolution and a three-dimensional look.

In this image, a small wooden dock extends over the surface of the lake. Seconds later, a white cottage materializes next to it. It looks like a summer home … one this man may have visited years ago. A childhood memory? No person appears in this scene, however. It is just a montage of water, sky, and cottage.

There's something hauntingly familiar, though, about that cottage. At first you can't put your finger on it, but then with a shiver you realize that it is the same cottage that recently appeared in one of your memory-dreams. Within that dream, you were a child sitting on the steps of a cottage facing a lake. Golden sunlight suffused the afternoon air. You blew a soap bubble and watched your face reflected on the shimmering surface of the sphere until it popped. Inexplicably, the image of the cottage in the visor must have come from *your* memory.

Seconds later fog engulfs the cottage and it vanishes.

Then another image appears — this one a pewter-toned face, like one in an old daguerreotype. The face belongs to an aristocratic-looking older woman wearing a balloon-sleeved blouse with a cameo pinned on the high starched collar. Her hair is tied back in a severe-looking bun. But in no time at all, this new image also vanishes — just as the image of the cottage did. After all this, you expect to see Ondine's face appear in the visor, but this does not happen.

Confused, you lean over the cot and whisper in his ear: "Who are you? Why are we here? Where do the images in the mask come from? Do you know?"

You don't have to think about saying this. The words just roll off your tongue. But the man lying on the cot still does not respond. You want him to be your guide, but so far he is just a human island, isolated, separate from you. His hand feels cold and looks quite old — thin, with bulging blue veins and so-called liver spots on the taut parchment skin. The only sound you hear is his rasping breathing and the murmuring surf outside.

Summoning every ounce of patience you have, you put your face close to the mask and repeat your question: "Who are you? Please tell me! I need to know!"

But he still doesn't respond, and no new clues appear on the glass.

As the icy edge of desperation creeps up your spine, you ask again, this time in a firmer voice: "Who are you? Why are we here? What's going on? Please … please … you must tell me!"

Again, the man on the cot makes no reply, and the visor covering his face darkens. Clenching your fists until your knuckles turn white, you say once more, as distinctly as you can, your voice now sounding hoarse: "I will ask you one more time: who ARE you? Why are we here? TALK TO ME!"

The man remains mute, insensate.

But now a few words appear on the surface of the visor:

HOME IS THE SAILOR, HOME FROM THE SEA

At this point the light within the massive glass jewel towering over the cot flares brightly. *Something important is happening now, but what?* All of a sudden you feel uncomfortable, as though you just intruded on a very intimate moment between the man on the cot and the light gleaming above him.

Should you be here now? Or should you leave?

Perplexed, you reluctantly descend the spiral staircase and return to your hotel room, where you find the frayed section of leather strap still lying on top of the dresser. Tomorrow you will see if it came from the strange mask on the lighthouse man.

Then something else on the dresser catches your eye: the needle on the compass is spinning wildly.

24

Early the next morning you race back to the lighthouse, hoping against hope that the man in the blue uniform has awakened and will cheerfully guide you out of Waves End. *After all, he must be here for a reason …*

The air has turned so frigid it makes your head ache, and the surf is raging higher than it has for days. Waves thunder against the jagged boulders below the lighthouse, spattering and swirling on the surface of the rocks. Freezing spray soaks you as you climb to the top of the promontory. When you reach the grassy surface and look down the coast, you notice that the reality-dissolving fog you spotted days ago has drifted alarmingly close to the Captain's Quay Hotel. Even the stars look fuzzy now, like tiny puffs of cotton. Then something almost makes you faint: the house called Sunrise Villa shimmers for a second and then disappears, having unburdened itself of Time.

The orange glow from the lighthouse gleams on the tombstones in the cemetery and the door of the lighthouse keeper's cottage still hangs open. It takes just a minute to run up the stairs to the lantern room.

But the cadaverous sea captain—or whatever he was—is gone now. All that remains of him is the peculiar mask lying on the cot, and the opalescent glow within the visor looks even dimmer than it did during your previous visit. What's more: instead of ghostly faces and dreamlike landscapes floating within the glass, black and white dots now wheel in complex fractal patterns—similar to the ones you saw in the toy spyglass and Ryder's microscope. These dots briefly merge into a sepia-toned image of a large house. But this image fades to a sketchy outline before you can study it. With a shudder you suspect that the light within the mask may not last much longer.

Then an extraordinary question pops into your mind: *Was the man in this tower a sentinel of some sort? A lone guard keeping watch over this crumbling edge of the continent?*

And the question that follows in the wake of this one stuns you like a lightning bolt:

Did you come here to replace him?

On a hunch, you take the section of leather strap you found in your room and hold it up to the lowermost strap on the mask. Sure enough, it matches; one more piece of the puzzle just snapped into place. Inside the visor are the engraved letters I.M.R. *Does the 'R' maybe stand for 'Ryder'? Do these letters say: "I am Ryder"?*

The visor has turned black, like a slab of onyx, and silver dragons of fog have begun to curl around the lighthouse, assuming fantastic and terrifying shapes. This monster fog is devouring everything in its path—even the brooding gables of the Captain's Quay Hotel. From this watchtower, all you can now see of the town are dark, misshapen silhouettes.

The mask feels surprisingly warm when you touch it. Oddly enough, this time when you examine the geometric symbols engraved on the brass rim, they begin to look familiar, as though they have somehow ignited a tiny spark of understanding. A voice inside you whispers: *Go ahead … put it on … you know you want to find out what it does …*

Galvanized by curiosity, you decide to put on the strange mask. Your hands shake as you slip it over your head, tugging on the leather bands until it fits snugly. Then you wait for a moment, expecting to be swept away, but nothing happens. The thing doesn't make you feel any different. Wondering if you *look* any different, you step closer to the glass panes of the wraparound window and study your reflection.

As you stand there, a sequence of images begins to flicker on the visor. With its silvery glass just a few inches away from the window, it's like two mirrors facing each other, multiplying the images in them into infinity. For a few seconds, the pale face of a haunted-looking young woman fills the glass. Then, moments later, the face of a man appears—perhaps a Spaniard, with dark pomaded hair and an olive complexion. Seconds after this, a Japanese Noh mask lights up the visor—the female character called Deigan, with her ghostly white face and golden eyes.

This is truly a mask of a thousand faces!

Could these images be more of your own memories welling up inside you? Could it even be that Waves End itself—its rocks and sand and weather-beaten houses—is fashioned out of pure memory … memories of a place you visited as a child … maybe even a place that was very important to you, a place that once felt magical?

And after all, is it not true that the Past is where we all live? For when something happens it takes a certain amount of time for the light to reach our eyes and a bit more time for the nerve impulses to travel from the eye to the brain. For us, the actual present moment is forever out of reach. And what can happen in that invisible zone between us and the real Present?

Suddenly, the lighthouse shudders in the wind and the storm panes around you creak unnervingly.

When you sit on the cot where the old man once lay, a new maelstrom of memories swirls just beyond your reach. The Fresnel lens has turned from amber to searing white and a dazzling cone of information-rich energy now beams from the tower, elucidating the night. Inside the lantern room, the light becomes so bright it hurts your eyes even through the visor.

And then, with a rumbling sound, the huge lens begins to rotate on the mercury flotation basin beneath it …

Amazingly, as the incandescent blade slashes through the darkness, the thick fog outside begins to dissipate. The land that was a smeary blur just minutes ago has regained its former clarity, and instead of looking like fuzzy disks, the stars once again sparkle like perfect diamonds.

Finally! This is what you've been waiting for: the lighthouse is finally pushing back the night!

You have the suspicion that your arrival here is what set the huge clockwork gears into motion. And this seems to confirm your earlier intuition:

YOU ARE THE NEW SENTINEL OF WAVES END!

Ironic, isn't it? All this time you've been trying to escape Waves End, but the truth is: you BELONG here. Your mind is lotus-ing into a brilliant beacon: its clear fire will soon light the way for lost sailors.

"But I'm not sure I can do that!" you protest, taking off the visor. "Shouldn't I get some training first? A few suggestions at least?"

No answer.

You suddenly feel desperately inadequate.

Being a sentinel here could be an onerous responsibility. At the end of the day, how would you even describe this town to someone? What words would you select? You could mention the stars, of course, and the surf and the darkness, but the silence between words would actually describe the place better.

And sadly you suspect that if the history of this miraculous event is ever recorded, the writing will eventually devolve into unintelligible runes in a diary no one will ever read. Or maybe the only evidence that you were here will be your name scrawled in a hotel guestbook. Such is often the fate of people who dare to think the unthinkable.

As you mull over these weighty thoughts, things in the lantern room become even stranger. The lens, the room, and the cot all develop a smoky red hue and become translucent. Ice crystals frost the windows. And then something *truly* bizarre happens: an enormous face appears outside the window, peering in at you. It is a man's face. He seems to be studying you. Gradually, through the sparkling ice, you make out more of this image. He is a middle-aged man with short pewter hair and a neatly-trimmed beard, wearing a white lab coat bearing the embroidered words "Methuselah Labs".

Voices murmur beyond the surf …

A young woman joins him. She also is wearing a white lab coat, and like the man, she is staring at you through the glass, her forehead creased with worry. Her face looks pallid in the antiseptic light from the LED panels in the ceiling.

"You're new here," the man says, turning to face her. "Your name again is—"

"Oops, I'm sorry, Doctor Ryder. I forgot to put on my nametag. It's Griffin ... Olivia Griffin."

"Welcome aboard, Doctor Griffin."

"Thank you, Sir."

"I believe you have been monitoring our guest here?"

"Yes, Sir."

She glances at a metal placard fixed below the window.

"Client 101-B," she reads out loud.

"That's correct."

Ryder strokes his beard and stares at you again through the window. His blue eyes look cold, analytical. Behind him stands a row of identical crystal sarcophagi inlaid with digital displays. Through the ice crystals, you see him frown.

"I don't know about this one," he says gravely. "This pod lost emergency power for several days. The chrysalises became dangerously warm. As you know, an uncontrolled thaw can prove fatal."

"But Doctor, the ice slurries have been bringing the temperature down rapidly. It's already thirty-two degrees inside the chrysalises. Maybe it's not too late."

"Hmn, we'll see ..."

He takes a pen-sized flashlight out of a pocket in his lab coat and shines it through the window of your chrysalis and through the windows of your eyes. The light is blinding; it looks like a star has gone supernova right in front of your face.

"The pupils don't dilate," he states clinically, jotting this observation down on a tablet computer. "What about the little girl next door?"

Griffin examines the display on the front of the chrysalis standing next to yours.

"Her wave patterns look entirely cryo-normal," she replies with relief.

"Good. It could be that her smaller body mass cooled down faster."

Next, Doctor Griffin presses a button on the display, sequencing through a series of screens showing columns of numbers and waveforms.

"This is interesting, Sir. Over the last few days her patterns occasionally resembled 101-B's. It's as though they became temporarily synchronized at an F-4 level of correlation."

"Really? Let me see …"

Ryder frowns and looks at the screen displaying the correlation matrix.

"Hmn," he says. "You're right. And those times coincide with the power surges we experienced when the emergency generators kicked in."

"Could some cross-talk have occurred between the two chrysalises?"

"I suppose that's possible. All the units here are connected to the same monitoring equipment. Can't say I've ever seen it happen though."

"How long will our nuclear batteries last?" Griffin asks, trying not to sound worried.

"Another few months, probably. We're putting quite a load on them down here."

Just at that moment a vibration ripples through the chamber, rattling the racks of instruments. Ryder glances apprehensively at the ceiling.

"That was a big one—"

"What was it, Sir?"

"A seismic wave from the surface. The missiles are getting closer."

"Sometimes I envy our clients," she remarks somberly. "Sleeping through all this."

He nods his head but says nothing.

"Sir," she says after a long pause, "I heard on the shortwave radio that some people are evacuating this sector."

He glances at her with a raised eyebrow.

"Is that what you want to do?"

"No," she whispers. "No … it's just that—"

"Doctor Griffin, you understand that we have a legal and moral obligation to preserve these people until a cure is found for their various maladies—even during wartime."

"Yes, Sir, I understand. I'm not thinking of leaving."

"I'm glad to hear that. And don't forget: this bunker is a thousand feet underground. It's probably the safest place to be right now."

"Yes, Sir. That *is* a comfort, of course."

"At any rate, we'll do what we can for these people. Please check 101-B's EEG again."

She glances at a large flat screen display mounted beside you. Her face looks soft and gentle, like a Raphael Madonna's. Firefly-green lights blink on a console behind her.

"What are you seeing now?"

"The frequency of the Delta waves just climbed to three hertz and the amplitude is increasing slightly."

"What about the Theta waves? Their frequency is critical for achieving the threshold of a cryo-state."

She studies the screen again.

"The frequency is holding at eight hertz but they're weak now … and growing weaker …"

"Any activity in the beta spectrum?

"Practically none."

"Theta at eight hertz," he repeats contemplatively. "The brain is now deeply immersed in a twilight state."

"I wonder what goes through their minds in there."

"Oh, I seriously doubt they're conscious."

"Doctor, I did my post-doc research on image-generation in stimulus-deprived brains."

"Doctor Griffin, these people aren't stimulus-deprived, they're *frozen.*"

"Uh-oh," she says with a frown, "look … a new anomaly just turned up in the Theta."

He steps in front of the display and studies it.

"Phase shift," he declares ominously.

"The frequency has fallen to four hertz," she notes quickly. "And the amplitude is attenuating fast. Oh, look … another phase shift—"

Squinting, he stares at the display for a moment.

"Yes, yes, I see it."

"Delta activity is now attenuating as well."

"Right," he replies with a resigned nod. "The required amplitude is no longer sustainable. I'm afraid it won't be long now."

Another surge of weightlessness buoys you up like a powerful tide, reclaiming you. *Do saints experience anything like this on the edge of their exquisite deaths?*

Suddenly weak, you lie down on the cot with the mask still strapped to your head. Outside the lighthouse-watchtower, the waves rolling in from the edge of infinity have become few and far between. Gripping both sides of the cot now, you brace for the breathtaking sensation of evanescence about to come.

The atoms of your mind begin to unlock.

Astonished, you watch yourself disintegrate and merge with the seascape around you:

Legs …

a lonely lighthouse … an arm … a rotating prism …

a dazzling cone of light …

a hand … a windswept beach …

another arm … a cemetery by the ocean …

waves rolling in below sparkling stars …

Until

THE END